AMERICAN POOL PLAYER
Make Every Shot Count

By
Calvin W. Maxwell, Jr.

Xulon PRESS

AMERICAN POOL PLAYER
Make Every Shot Count
by Calvin W. Maxwell, Jr.

Printed in the United States of America

ISBN 9781622301416

www.xulonpress.com

For my family,

my boyhood memories and

James "Cisero" Murphy

Table of Contents

Chapter 1

The Game

September 1984

*I*t was 4am in the morning and I couldn't sleep. I fluffed my pillow, turned to my other side and tried to go back to dream land. In a few hours I would be off to my first day of high school and I could feel the anxiety pressing down on my soul. I stared at the wall in front of me and glanced up at the wooden crucifix just above my bed in the darkness. I wondered if Jesus really knew me and if he would truly guide me through. I was just a young freshman who loved playing pool, nothing more. There were so many troubles in the world, why would Jesus take time for me I thought. – I quickly perked up and put my slippers on. I walked into the bathroom, turned on the light, ran warm water on my washcloth and wiped my face and neck. I looked in the mirror. "Am I unique or special in the eyes of God," I asked myself. I didn't hear an answer. I turned the bathroom light off, went back into my room and quietly shut the door. I turned my light on, threw on my imaginary cowboy hat and went inside my bottom dresser draw were I kept my books. I pulled out my bible, re-read a few passages from Psalms and thought about playing pool in the basement of Mr. Evan's house. Afterwards, I pretended my fingers were pistols and had a show-down with my shadow. It was now five minutes after five and I could feel my anxiety shift. My eyes finally began to close. I was back in dream land...

Well, Grice Grafton, it's off to another town I reckon. Hopefully, this one will be better than the last one. "With the good Lord by my side, I ain't dyin' in Northside County and I ain't takin' no gruff either," I thought quietly as I swatted away the buzzing insects from my sweat-soaked cowboy hat. Even the butt of my gold-plated Smith & Wesson cue stick was warm from the desert heat. My horse needed water and I was still miles from...

RIINNNGGGG!!

The alarm clock woke me up. My mother put my new clothes

and sneakers on top of my dresser. My haircut still looked fresh and I did a few push-ups for extra measure. My first day at Northside High School was about to begin and all I wanted was to play pool. The pressure was on and my mind began to wander again.

As a child, I loved to shoot pool with Mr. Evans, the landlord who kept a small well-kept billiards table in his basement. Mr. Evans was a friendly, semi-retired welder who enjoyed going to church, but was a real billiards enthusiast at heart. Mr. Evans loved talking about his childhood in segregated Norfolk, Virginia and how he use to hustle for money in the pool halls. He taught me how to pocket bank shots, make combination shots (sometimes called caroms), and to never, ever forget to chalk-up before each approach. "It's the small details of one's game that make all the difference", he would say – winning any game due to dumb luck was winning without honor. However and perhaps most importantly, strategizing any type of victory requires confidence in one's own abilities and building confidence requires studying and practicing one's trade. Everyone has small weaknesses in their game, even the all-time greats, but confidence can fill in the void and intimidate opponents.

A strong defensive game is also crucial. No matter how talented or skilled, no one can win without confidence and defense. Protecting yourself from shark bites is key. I learned all those game enriching lessons from Mr. Evans and some on my own, just as I'm sure he knew I would.

My parents didn't mind me playing pool every afternoon as long as my homework was always done and my grades didn't meager. I think my parents were proud of the fact that I took such an effortless interest in a sport that didn't have any remote possibility of concussions or broken bones. Besides, I really didn't have much of an appetite for boxing gloves or shoulder pads. From the time I was 9 to 14 years-old, I would play 8-ball, 9-ball, or straight pool almost every day with Mr. Evans or his youngest son Roy or even sometimes my Dad would play when he didn't have to work overtime. I studied the legends of the game, like Willie Mosconi, Minnesota Fats, Ralph Greenleaf, Jimmy Moore, Luther Lassiter, Steve Mizerak, and Mike Sigel. I wanted to absorb all I could about those who achieved prominence in the cue arts. I was particularly interested in any great black players. Were there any? Yes. His name was Cisero Murphy and he stood toe-to-toe with the best pool players of his era. He was a champion who played the game with intelligence, class and he never forgot where he came from. Other than my father and Mr. Evans, Cisero Murphy became one of my early boyhood heroes.

When I turned 14, everything that was essential to my normal pool playing world would completely change. My parents were now able to buy a home of their own further uptown, thanks to all the overtime my father worked, and my folks weren't about to convert valuable cellar space into a billiards parlor just to motivate my foolish efforts of a winning some national pool championship. That's all I ever dreamed about. I was now a freshman in high school and all I thought about was becoming my generation's Cisero Murphy. Now... I had new classmates, new rules to follow , and a new group of bullies to avoid. It hurt knowing that Mr. Evans was no longer in my life on an everyday basis. For the first time in my life I was forced into thinking about other things like cars, money, and girls. I was about to be bombarded with new annoying teachers, tons of homework, decisions to make...billiards came easy to me and I needed to shoot a few racks...

and fast!

In school we're told to keep strict adherence and even try to live up to the philosophical teachings of Dr. King and 'the reformed' Malcolm X. In the famous "I Have a Dream" speech – Dr. King passionately and eloquently states that he longs for a day when the children of former slaves and the children of former slave owners could hold hands and skip into the sunset. Was that realistic? Should the descendants of those who were wounded by slavery ever trust the descendants of those who inherited financial benefit from slavery? Could the children of former slave owners completely respect the children of those they conquered? Fighting to hold hands is one thing --- fighting for trust, respect, spiritual reconciliation, business development and intellectual balance in America is something different all together – that requires real work and commitment from both the elite and the defeated. Was Christianity still the answer? Was it still relevant in my neighborhood? For many young, impressionable black men, we were ready to listen and follow a new progressive voice, one that the white man didn't easily approve of and Nation of Islam Minister Louis Farrakhan was a fresh faced, strong postured leader who gave the black pride movement new muscle and a deeply felt dose of straight talk. As far as many were concerned at that time this was the voice of my generation!

I was never a so-called street kid, but I knew that my environment needed new direction. My city was never perfect but it was beginning to show the signs of real physical decay and neglect. Thanks to President Ronald Reagan and his dismantling of important government programs, I could see and feel the frustration and battle-wiriness in the faces of my community. I could interpret the body language and some of the slang. The desegregation policy victories of the Civil Rights Era allowed the best and brightest of the black community to attend the best schools in white neighborhoods and move into the sanctuary of the suburbs. Even the most hardcore militant black people needed a solid 9-5 to support their families. The magnificent symphony of thoughtful grassroots adult leadership like W.E.B. Du Bois and Medger Evers was now being replaced with the sounds of disenfranchised youth. A hard working blue-collar father's decade long sweat to earn a better life for his family seemed misguided when a man could make fast money on the streets. Selling drugs became the new black fist.

Dealers were driving fancy European cars and turning the heads of sexy, green-eyed women. That fact, I believe, broke the hearts of many good working class American black men. Men like my father and Mr. Evans. Many were made to feel like they were suckers. Why should an honest man work extra hours and weekends, when a street-wise thug could make thousands on the corner? I knew the truth, though. The honest dollar earning black men of my city were the true kings. Too bad there wasn't any leadership to shout those words aloud into a megaphone on Dr. King's mountaintop. – When a tree falls in the forest and no one is around to hear it...the sound it makes is inconsequential.

At age 14, music became one of my closest friends and hip-hop was my Ginger Rogers. I kept my most prized cassettes all in a giant shoe box on a shelf just above my bed. The box was packed with Kurtis Blow, Afrika Bambaata, Grandmaster Flash & the Furious Five, Run-DMC, and Whodini. My dream of becoming a pool legend was still burning brightly and I knew I could beat almost anyone on any pool table. I desperately wanted to prove that this kid who spent the early years sinking reverse bank shots had the credentials and skills to be 'The King of Rock'!

Chapter 2

Radicals

*T*hroughout my high school years I also listened to many speeches by Minister Farrakhan, who some labeled a radical. Who defines the word 'radical'? From my point of view, I didn't think Farrakhan was as radical as the people that bought Africans to America as slaves and kept them there for 300 years. I didn't think he was as radical as racism or police brutality. I agreed with the magniloquent Farrakhan when he said black men should respect themselves, start businesses, study their own history, and treat black women as precious gems. How could any reasonable person be against 'The Minister' if he's speaking for the upliftment of a people who are among the poorest and weakest of a country that proclaims 'and justice for all'? My faith in Jesus still burned brightly, but the strong opposition to Farrakhan from the establishment only made him more intriguing. Throughout my youth I read the bible and listened to Farrakhan. I wasn't sure of what to believe exactly, so I became all sonar.

The whole school experience itself isn't exactly "Chopsticks" on a piano anyway, but graduating from middle school into high school is a cruel demotion. It's a descent into the fiery abyss of zits, insecurity, and countless awkward moments. Those who can play football, sing popular R&B songs, or make others laugh, are the cool kids. There are no pool tables in high school. No snooker teams to join. Girls don't read Billiards Digest or talk about that cool dude with that fine leather cue case! My best skills were as useless as putting fur coat on a grizzly bear. I was the coolest invisible kid in my high school and it was my classmate's lost in not knowing so!! My confidence as a pool player was in direct conflict with my social ranking as a dorky freshman. "I could beat anyone in this school at pool", I thought quietly. "8 ball, 9 ball, straight pool, it didn't matter. Dear God, please just give me that chance. I'll show them! I'll show them all!!"

RIINNNGGGG!!

Northside High School wasn't all mysterious faces though. I recognized a few friends and foes. There was Kevin "Knowledge Born" Dalton, a friend I made at Heritage Baptist Church Summer Camp while in junior high school. He was a big boned dark-skin kid from the better section of town that gave himself the name "Knowledge Born" after learning that many black Americans had inherited the same surnames as their former slave owners. "Knowledge" and I both enjoyed listening to Minister Farrakhan, reading comic books, watching sports and discussing cultural philosophy. I've only played Knowledge a few times on the pool table- I'll get to that later. Next, there was "Big Mouth" Brenda Barnes, the most popular girl at my old elementary school, the class valedictorian and my next door neighbor from when I lived in the Evans house. It was a fact that Brenda could out talk most school teachers and couldn't keep a single secret. She didn't give herself her nickname, she simply earned it!

Western Civilization, English Composition, Science, Gym and Algebra class everyday weren't the only obstacles. Northside High

School was travelling at spine twisting warp speed in comparison to middle school. And no one cares if you pass, fail or die. There are no pacifiers or teething rings in high school – it's all up to you. Upperclassmen are too busy ignoring freshmen to concern themselves with anything less than their own personal status. What was my father like in high school, I wondered. What was Mr. Evans like as a kid? Could Jesus survive high school? I knew that my idol, Cisero Murphy, was a high school dropout at age 15 and become the New York City pool champion at age 16. My parents would literally kill me if I even thought about dropping out of school. To them, education was the best path to reach the King-ian mountaintop. -- What were my own high school years going to become? There is no workshop or seminar on how a student can survive high school. I knew my fate was in my own hands and I tried to let my imagination flow like a nice break during the beginning of a competitive pool match. Life is no fun without daydreams. They can forecast inspirational light inside the dark cave of uncertainty.

As a freshman, I tried to remember all the little lessons Mr. Evans taught me about playing pool. For example, every great pool player must have an appetite for winning. Without the component of hunger, the potential for positive results severely diminish. However, what was I trying to win at Northside? Is it possible to win at high school the way a pool hustler can win a satchel of cash? My only appetite on my first day of high school was for self-preservation. Little did I know just how many thorny hurtles were going stand in my way.

Chapter 3

"Friendship"

"**W**hat's up, Knowledge?" I said as I saw my friend in the auditorium during freshman orientation.

"Yo, G-Man, what's uuuup, man?!" a smiling Knowledge replied as we embraced.

"I'm good, man. Have you seen some of the fine honeys in this place?"

"Oh, yeah! I'm working on gettin' some digits now! Hahaaaaa! We're in high school, G-man! We're going to make Northside shine, ya heard?!"

"Did you get your schedule in the mail? Let's see if we have some of the same classes."

Knowledge digs in his back pocket. "Yeah. Gimme your schedule,

G-man," Knowledge said softer. "Let's see what we got here. Yeah, we both got gym class 5th period and our choice of shop class the last two periods of 8th and 9th. What shop you gonna take, G-man?"

"I'm not completely sure. I signed on for welding..."

"No, G-man. Take electronics like me, bro. That's what the brothers have got to get into, for real. Electronics is the future. THAT'S what's up!"

"Yeah?"

"Yeah! Why welding? If you can do math, you can do electronics! It's as simple as that. "

"Alright. That sounds...yeah, I'll, I'll take a look at electronics."

"You sure, G-man?"

"I'm sure. I just never thought seriously about electronics before, but I did get straight A's in math, so..."

"Bet, bro. I think we should sit down. The principal just got on the mic. Let's go over here."

"Ok."

RIINNNGGGG!!

As the principal, Mrs. Brunswick took to the auditorium stage and force fed a longwinded speech to the incoming freshman class about embarking on new endeavors, taking personal responsibility, ending gang violence, preventing teen suicide, saying no to drugs, studying early for the SATs, eating fruits and vegetables, getting a good-night's sleep, ending bullying, attending classes on time, joining after school programs, participating in sports, embracing abstinence, maintaining good grades, staying out of trouble, preparing for college, respecting all educators, and living a life of purpose, we were all ready for the firing squad! Any type of adventurous outlook that was ready to illuminate within our spirits at the entrance of Northside, home of the 'Mighty Lions', was completely crushed like someone's neck in a headlock applied by Hulk Hogan! Was this really 'high' school? Rules, rules, and more rules. I had the funny feeling that most of us freshmen were in for unprecedented disappointment during our reign here. Go, go, lions, go...grrr.

As Mrs. Brunswick closed her speech by saying "smile and the world will smile with you," Knowledge and I quickly said our see-you-laters and scattered in different directions to find our 2nd period classes. My first period Sociology class with Mrs. Ball would have to wait until the next day, I guess. I now had West Civilization with Mr. Connelly who looked like he was a hippie back in his hay day. He was relaxed and self assured in his ability. He reminded me of my dad a little, the way he spoke with his hands and all while teaching. Was it possible, that for the first time in my life I might actually enjoy learning from the white man's history book? Just because it was HIS story didn't mean I couldn't learn valuable lessons from it, I thought quietly.

"My style of teaching is primarily oral", Mr. Connelly stated calmly while sitting behind his desk, "I will rarely write on the chalkboard, so, my expectation... is that you will pay attention...use positive communication...for your grade in class participation, which is essential. I believe everyone will not only pass...but get an A in my class." All the students looked at each other half smiling and I thought "Wow", a white teacher using poetry/hip-hop in a classroom introduction. This old hippie history teacher is kind of...sort of cool.

"As I go around the room, row by row, you are to state your name, your personal career goals and one fact about western history, beginning with you...remember, anything about Western Civilization that is spoken about in this class will be on your weekly tests given every Thursday." As Mr. Connelly motioned to the cute nervous light-skin girl in a bright red blouse directly to his right, all the students began fumbling around for notebooks and pens.

"My name is Jennifer Gooden. I want to be a nurse. And, um… George Washington… was… the first president of the United States?" Many of the students erupted with laughter.

"Will you be taking part in the nursing program offered at Northside, Jennifer?" Asked Mr. Connelly as he checked off her name in his attendance book and wrote a few notes.

"Yes," Jennifer Gooden said firmly.

"Super. Now as far as George Washington is concerned…yes he was the first president. He was also a British general, was involved in the Battle of Waterloo, and the American Revolution."

Students were writing franticly.

"Next, please."

"My name is Hector Velasquez. I'm taking Business because I want help my dad with his vending machine business. What I know about western history is that the Statue of Liberty was a gift from

France back in, um …"

"Yes. The artist who created the design of the statue is… Auguste… Bartholdi. The statue, which is made of copper, was placed in pieces in crates and put on a ship called the SS Isere. That ship left for America in mid 1884 and later reassembled here… and dedicated on October 28, 1886. Does anyone remember the famous poem Emma Lazarus wrote called 'Mother of Exiles' about the Statue of Liberty???"

The class was rushing to keep up.

"Give me your tired, your poor huddled masses yearning to be free…"

"Good memory. What's your name?"

"Grice Grafton."

"Give me your tired, your poor,

Your huddled masses yearning to breathe free,

The wretched refuse of your teeming shore.

Send these, the homeless, tempest-tost, to me,

I lift my lamp beside the golden door!"

"Yeah. That's it." Some of the students sighed and smirked.

"What is your career goal, Grice?" Mr. Connelly threw me for a loop with that one. I was supposed to be the twelfth student picked.

"I want to be a great pool champion." Some chuckled and I could feel the perplexed looks in the room. Someone even said, "Did he say pool cleaner?"

"Can you play?" asked Mr. Connelly.

"I can beat anyone. I'm the best," I said. Protest and sneers erupted. I could feel my ventral prefrontal cortex snap in half.

"Quiet down. -- Well, Grice, don't let anyone or anything stop you from achieving your goals. A healthy dose of hubris can be a great thing, but just because you maybe 'the best' at something, doesn't mean you should brag or become complacent either. Keep practicing and fighting for your dream young man. Thank you," Mr. Connelly said with a slight nod and wink. And with those words, the class was calm again. Mr. Connelly had a great way of successfully calibrating the right tone for the class. He was a proud Buddhist and rarely yelled at students or seemed unprepared. He had real effortless style like Mr. Evans was at a pool table. Mr. Connelly would go on to become one of my favorite teachers.

Chapter 4

Teachers

W estern Civilization class went quick. Only half the students got to introduce themselves, say what their goals were, and give some well-known fact about American history. Most of the students gave normal career goals like police officer, optometrist, physician, auto mechanic, archaeologist, car designer, beautician, museum curator, or train conductor. I was surprised that so many of the career choices weren't even offered as shop options at Northside. Some girl even said she wanted to be "a clair-voyant." I didn't feel so bad about my choice after I heard that. The other half of the class would have their anxiety related disorders put on full display the following day.

RIINNNGGGG!!

It was now the beginning of 3rd period which meant it was English Composition time. Mrs. Slate was our tormenter.

"GET IN HERE, take a seat, TAKE out a piece of PAPER, a pen, NO PENCIL and shut it... PRONTO!!" she shouted. "You will WRITE your FULL name at the top LEFT-hand corner...WRITE today's date at the top RIGHT-hand corner. After THAT, you will WRITE the words: English Composition just below your NAME and write MY NAME, Mrs. S-L-A-T-E just below today's date. I WROTE an example on the board. YOUR TOPIC IS: My Hero. You are to AT LEAST write a complete PAGE detailing who YOUR hero IS and WHY THIS person is important TO YOU. You are to write QUIETLY and neatly. BEGIN!"

"I don't have a pen," one boy said.

"That's not MY problem," said Mrs. Slate' "I get PAID whether you're prepared or NOT!" Just then a kindhearted classmate reached into their pencil case and handed the unprepared boy a brand new Bic.

"My pastor is my hero. Can I write about my pastor?" a familiar enthusiastic voice asked. I looked pass the chubby kid to my right and it was none other than my nemesis, the evil "Big Mouth"

Brenda Barnes. I thought I was going regurgitate my morning cinnamon raisin bagel.

"Yes," said Mrs. Slate answering Brenda's suck up question.

As I briefly glanced at Brenda, I couldn't help but wonder what horror would be uncoiled in the days, weeks, and months that lie ahead. She was writing about Pastor McDonaldson of Heritage Baptist Church just to score snuggle points with Mrs. Slate. That was crystal clear! Someone needs to stop her! It's only the first day and "Big Mouth" Brenda is already scheming, plotting and working the system to her advantage. Northside High School just met Brenda and they haven't the slightest idea of what she's truly capable of. Everyone should starting running from the girl that can spew lava from her larynx and electromagnetic gases from her eye sockets.

I wasn't going to play safety though. I was going to go for the tougher shot. "Chalk it up, line it up, and sink it," as Mr. Evans would say. I could write about Dr. King, Paul Laurence Dunbar, A. Philip Randolph, George Washington Carver, Ralph Bunche or Jackie Robinson...they were on America's acceptable Negro hero list. Or I could write about *agape theou* which means God's love for man.

I've memorized some of my favorite passages that give evidence of God's everlasting love. For example, in Ephesians 2: 4-5 it states "But because of his great love for us, God, who is rich in mercy, made us alive with Christ even when we were dead in transgressions-- it is by grace you have been saved." I learned so many lessons at Heritage Baptist Church I could definitely write a whole paper on that. Then I thought that was way too existential. I didn't want to violate the First Amendment of separation of church and state on my very first writing assignment in high school. There were many tactics to approach this paper with I suppose. The acceptable and religious I ruled out for the moment. Maybe the hardcore approach was best. I'm a proud black kid that wants engage real thought-provoking militant dialogue. I wanted to write about Minister Louis Farrakhan, but he was still fairly new to me and I didn't know enough about him to write a full page at that time. I would learn more about 'The Minister' later and that would eventually lead to an interesting discussion in Mr. Connelly's class.

The first time I met Knowledge was during the Heritage Baptist Church Summer Camp. He let me keep his book about Malcolm X in which I read in one sitting. I really wanted to write Malcolm X's brutally honest assessment of racism in America, "I'm not going to sit at your table and watch you eat, with nothing on my plate, and call myself a diner....Sitting at the table doesn't make you a diner...Being here in America doesn't make you an American." I could feel Mrs. Slate's steely blue eyes perching down. I started to sweat cue balls and rethink my choice. Would writing about Farrakhan or Malcolm X get me in trouble? People in authority can be funny sometimes. I remembered Mr. Evans talking about how a defense can be a great offense. I didn't want to create total entropy on my first day at Northside. I know... I'll write about Cisero Murphy. After all he was a pool player and he really was my hero!

"No TIME for lolly-gagging, only 30 MINUTES LEFT YOUNG MAN," yelled Mrs. Slate, waving her pointer finger over my paper which only had my name, date, English Composition, and Medusa's other name. Time was deteriorating fast. I needed to start writing. I was skeptical of my own decision to write that a little known pool legend, Cisero Murphy was my hero, but I sized up Mrs. Slate and wanted to build up some good equity with her. Maybe the uniqueness of my choice would show her how creative I was. Pool was always my passport to a harmoniously fame-filled trophy-hoisting all-the-beautiful-girls-love-me future anyway and this writing assignment was no exception. My friend "Knowledge" would be a little disappointed that I didn't go full tilt militant, but he'll never find out, so-what-the-hay. Besides Knowledge didn't know diddley about pool - We played a couple of racks of 8-ball at Captain Sam's Arcade last year and I vaporized Knowledge so badly he never wanted to play me again. He said pool was for people who couldn't play a real sport. But he was just sore that I could beat him at something. Knowledge had to acknowledge my gift, like it or not. - My dad and Mr. Evans would be proud of my choice for this paper, I'd bet.

My Hero: Cisero

My hero, other than my parents, is James "Cisero" Murphy who was the first black-American professional pool player to win a world or U.S. billiards title. He was one of eight children and grew up in the hard knocks Bedford-Stuyvesant part of Brooklyn, New York. His dad left the family when Cisero was young and his mom was left with no choice but to go on welfare. When Cisero was 15, he dropped out of high school and began playing pool at the Police Athletic League (PAL). He loved playing pool and practiced every chance he could.

Cisero Murphy won the New York City Championship at age sixteen and become the State Champion five years after that. From 1959 to 1964, Cisero also won the Eastern State Championship in the PAL. Sadly, because Cisero was a black man in an era where racial tensions were still harsh, he was never invited to compete for a world title until 1965 despite his extraordinary skills. In 1965 though, after finally being given an opportunity on a larger stage (many protested his exclusion previously); James "Cisero" Murphy defeated iconic white players such as Jimmy Moore and Luther Lassiter to win the Burbank World Invitational. – Some people have compared Cisero Murphy to Jackie Robinson for helping to break the color barrier and dispel certain stereotypes in sports.

In his later years, Cisero Murphy now visits veteran hospitals and senior citizen homes to give trick shot exhibitions and educate people about how to play pool. Cisero Murphy is my hero because he's a great pool player champion who fought and overcame many obstacles.

-Time was up. - My masterpiece was complete. Mrs. Slate will love my paper. I'd bet it's the best slice of miniature literature ever written. I waited to give my submission because I wanted mine to be on top. There, done!

RIINNNGGGG!!

I quickly looked at my schedule and 4th period was Science with Mr. Bassford in Room #303 which was on the third floor.

"Hey, Bagel Boy," a voice from behind me said. I knew who it was instantly. It was Big Mouth Brenda.

"Don't start with that Bagel Boy stuff or I'm going tell Pastor McDonaldson that your soul can't ever be saved."

"Oh, stop that! You know I like busting your chops! Where are you headed?"

"Science. Room #303."

"I have Earth Science in #305. Let's walk together."

"Alright."

"You remember we use to walk to School #20 together

sometimes with Juan and Samantha? I always cracked jokes on you. You were always so quiet, though."

"Not all the time, but yeah...I, I remember that. What happened to the twins?"

"I think they go to Roberto Clemente High School, now. Anyway, Mr. Evans asked about you and your parents the other day. Where did your family move to? Are you still going to attend Heritage?"

"I don't really know. My mom thinks..."

"Oh, there's my home girls. Thanks for the walk. Good luck in high school, Bagel Boy," Brenda said with an evil grin.

"Good luck in psychotherapy, Big Mouth." It was the first time I ever called Brenda that out loud. Brenda was called "Big Mouth" before by a great many people, but never by me. She deserved it! I wasn't going take it any longer.

"Oh, my God! I don't believe you," Brenda said as she turned back. "I'm going to get you back for that," she said as her small brown finger poked my chest before she disappeared into the crowd.

The day was still young and I was feeling hungry and tired. I hope Science class produces some stimuli to my brain's dopamine.

Mr. Bassford was a tall wiry man who wore heavy bifocals, a white lab coat and had a nervous twitch in his left eye. He was late to his own class. He also brought a shopping cart filled with folders, jars, and plastic bins with him.

"Please stop talking. Thank you. My name is Mr. Bassford. Welcome to Northside High School and welcome to Science. There will be assigned seating, so don't get too comfortable. As a matter of fact, I would appreciate everyone standing up with all your belongings. Thank you. As I call your name, you will sit at your assigned table. There are eight tables as you can see. Each table is clearly numbered and there will be no more than 4 students at each table. No one, I repeat, no one is allowed to go into the lab area without authorization. Is that totally clear? I appreciate that. Thank you. There is no shouting, no eating, no running, no foul language, and absolutely no horseplay of any kind in this class. Is that understood? Thank you. You will speak when spoken to. You will complete all assignments in a time efficient manner and all work will be kept neat. I have labeled science folders for each student. After you receive your folder you will write your name and class period on that label. There is a syllabus inside each labeled folder explaining testing times of this class and my grading system. You will leave your labeled folders in the corresponding colored bins which are also numbered by the window sill, here. As I call your name, you will grab a colored labeled folder from the shopping cart that directly corresponds with the number and color on each table and go to that table quietly. Thank you for your cooperation. Now, I would appreciate it if all students would move to the right side of the classroom, forming a straight line. There is still no talking. I said QUIET! Thank you. Nehalem Anderson, please step forward. You will be at table #1 which is blue, so please grab a blue labeled folder from the cart and sit at the appropriate table. Please don't forget that your numbered blue labeled folder will go in the blue bin of the same number before you leave my classroom. Thank you. Next, Germ Bailey, please step forward. You will be at table #2 which is red, so please grab the red labeled folder from the cart…"

By the time all of us students were seated in our groups at the assigned tables and put our personalized colored and numbered labeled folders in there correct colored and numbered bins, the bell that signals the end of 4th period had rang. Mr. Bassford continued talking.

"I have a reward system that I feel you should be made aware of before you leave. Please settle down. Settle down I said! I will let you go momentarily. Thank you. I have eight labeled and numbered clear jars that correspond with each table that everyone is sitting at. Every day of each marking period that your group is successful at an assignment, I will place a colored marble in the appropriate labeled and numbered jar that directly corresponds with each numbered table that has the same color. The table that receives the most marbles at the end of each marking period will win a special science prize. Is that understood? Are there any questions? Thank you. Enjoy the rest of your day." Every student bolted from that science room as if we were being chased by a pack of zombie mountain goats.

RIINNNGGGG!!

It was now 5th period, which meant it was gym time! The gymnasium was in the basement on the other side of the Joseph P. Torello, Jr. Building. I had to move fast to prevent from being extremely late as opposed to being a little bit late. I hope Mr. Bassford doesn't keep us after the bell every day! I hate being late.

The traffic in the hallway was intense. Kids were everywhere, pushing, yelling and pointing out the physical flaws and poor fashion choices of others. Security guards were trying to orchestrate some sense of order. I could see Mrs. Brunswick, the principal, yelling at some students for running. I just knew I was going to be the last student in the gymnasium.

Ms. Gomez was my gym teacher. She was 5 feet tall, had short Pat Benatar-like hair, and beautiful tan legs the size of gas tanks on an 18 wheeler. She definitely didn't seem like the type of person that you would bet against if she fought a Mongolian warrior.

"I know that some of you will be late for various reasons and as long as you come prepared with shorts, sneakers, and a good attitude I'm willing to overlook the small stuff. If you don't come prepared or you give me any problems in terms of poor sportsman-ship, not following the rules or a bad attitude, you will receive a failing grade. Now, I don't expect every student to be the next Larry Bird, Magic Johnson or Carl Lewis, but I do expect you to try. As a matter of fact, that is my motto: I WILL TRY! As an entire class repeat..."

"I WILL TRY!"

"Say it again..."

"I WILL TRY!"

"Louder!"

"I WILL TRY!!!!"

"Now, there are no short-shorts, low cut blouses or tank tops to be worn in this class. I prefer that all sneakers be high-tops to protect ankles. Absolutely no jewelry is to be worn in gym. Sweat bands are okay. The locker room areas are where you will change and use the bathroom. Boys go to the Boy's Locker Room to the right. Girls go to the Girl's Locker Room which is located to the left. I'm pleased to see that most of the class is wearing sneakers. Those who didn't come prepared, please sit in the bleacher area. Those of you that are ready line up on the black line."-- I could see Knowledge at the other side of the gym with a different gym teacher who was giving the same rules as Ms. Gomez. I was starting to worry about changing my shop class from welding to electronics. Mr. Evans had a lot of connections in the welding field which I could easily take advantage of. Besides, I knew what welding was. I wasn't exactly sure of what electronics was. Was changing my shop class even a good idea? Did God want me to go into electronics? I needed to make a decision.

"Ms. Gomez. Can I please go to the office to change my shop major", I asked firmly.

"What's your name?"

"Grice Grafton."

"Let me just... check you off. Sure, go ahead. Just make sure to come prepared for gym tomorrow. And bring a combination lock for your gym locker. Good luck."

"Thanks, Ms. Gomez," I was surprised as to how wholesticly cool Ms. Gomez was. I quickly grabbed my backpack and walked as fast as I could to the main office.

As I passed through the hallway I noticed that the Electronics shop class wasn't too far from the gymnasium. I had to peek inside. Instructor R. Torello was written on the chalkboard. I wondered if he was related to Joseph P. Torello, Jr. whose name was etched in steel on the front of the very building in which I stood. The instructor was a tough looking guy with a bald head, a curly handle bar mustache, and an obvious limp. "Ohm's Law" was written in heavy yellow chalk in the upper left side of the board along with some words I've never seen.

– DC Bridges, Wheatstone Bridges, Potentiometer Bridges, Thevinen's Theorem, Symmetrical Wheatstone Bridges, and Series to Parallel Conversion were just some of the words bullet pointed with equations and rectangular diagrams held together by dots- they reminded me of pockets on a pool table. There were zigzags and squiggly lines going through the diagrams with letters beside them. There were upperclassmen sitting at work stations with dis- assembled computers. I could feel a rush of electricity go through my body like current through an open transistor. I was now in high school and I could make decisions for myself.

The whole reason I originally wanted to attend Northside and not Roberto Clemente or The Henry O. Tanner High School of Arts, which were considered the top choices in my area, was to become a welder like Mr. Evans who was like a grandfather to me.

He learned welding in the Navy and always seemed happy with his career choice. My dad worked long hours all the time and Mr. Evans was always there for friendly and at times not-so-light-hearted conversion about race, politics, sports, and women. Sometimes I would shoot pool or play basketball in the backyard with Mr. Evans' youngest son Roy who was 20 years old and didn't seem to do much other than listen to his boom box. Mr. Evans' older son Rod followed his dad to become a Navy man himself and Mr. Evans was extremely proud to show anyone pictures of him in uniform. I enjoyed Mr. Evans' easy going Christian style and slight southern drawl. What I loved about him was his sniper-like accuracy as a pool player. I wanted to play the game just like him.

I hurried to the Main Office to change my major from Welding to Electronics, second guessing myself the whole way. Was I switching my major for the right reasons? Was I right to follow my friend Knowledge's advice about Electronics being the future? As I spoke with the school secretary, then my guidance counselor and even as I was signing the paper to switch, I thought I might be making a mistake; I went against my gut instinct for the first time in my life and switched anyway.

It was almost the beginning of 6th period, which meant it was just about lunch time. I was going invade the cafeteria like a starving Red-tailed Hawk about to drop down on a small rodent. I was also hoping that high school café food was a step up from elementary school road kill. Those hopes were quickly and significantly thwarted. On the menu: soggy chicken tacos, half-cooked carrots, syrupy peaches and your choice of milk. Yum.

The cafeteria seemed as big as an aircraft hangar. The cafeteria staff members weren't smiling airline stewardesses either. I was going to be the first guinea pig for the first lunch of my freshmen class; the least they could've done was supply me with a complimentary barf bag. With lunch time being so late in the day though, that taco and carrots tasted like filet mignon. I wanted to wait for Knowledge but I knew he would be late from gym class. He was almost always late. By the time he arrived and sat across from me in the café, I was finishing my milk.

"What happen to you in gym, G-man?"

"I went to the office to change my shop major to Electronics."

"That's my boy! 'Supreme Mathematics' that's what's up. -- Yo, G-man. Check out that fly honey at your 9 o'clock."

I looked to my far left at the next table and saw Shonelle, one of "Big Mouth" Brenda's evil cronies from School #20. She didn't even know I was alive. Knowledge thought any girl with big boobs was a fly chick. Shonelle was a girl who wore glasses and was slightly buck toothed from all her past thumb sucking.

"Yeah. She looks alright."

"You're crazy, G-man. Look at that rack. I'd get those digits in a minute."

As soon as Knowledge said the word 'rack' I immediately thought about all the different kinds of racks there are in pool. Wooden racks, plastic racks, diamond shaped racks just for 9-ball…

"What's up, Knowledge Born," said 'Big Mouth' Brenda as she snuck up behind me, smushed the back of my head and stuck her tongue out in my direction.

"What's popping, Breezy?"

"Nothing. You should watch the company you keep, Knowledge Born. I hear incurable dweebiness is contagious."

"Who? G-man? That's my man right here!!"

"Shut up you haggard witch from the glaciers of Malaria Mountain," I said firmly.

"Oooooo, Bagel Boy, does your mother, who I know by the way, know that you speak this way to good Christian girls?"

"Does your mother know that you wear a black pointy hat at night and can convert any broomstick into a lunar module?"

"Don't try to besmirch my good name, Bagel Boy of Dorkville. You're just trying to impress Knowledge."

"Is it true that the International Committee of Witches has considered voting hang gliders safer than brooms?"

I could see Knowledge holding back tears as he wolfed down his chicken taco and harpooned his milk carton with a straw.

"Anyway," said 'Big Mouth' Brenda as she showed me her right palm, "Knowledge, were you able to jot down the American History homework? Mrs. Campbell's handwriting is atrocious."

'Yeah, Breezy. I'll give it to you right after I'm done eating. -- I didn't know you knew my boy, Breezy."

"Yeah. We go waaayy back. Right, Bagel Boy?"

"Unfortunately."

"Well y'all, I gotta go to my people. I'll catch you later, Knowledge Born. – And to you Bagel Boy, I love hang gliding," said 'Big Mouth' Brenda as she walked away with a long sly wink.

"Fly safely," I said.

Chapter 5

Brenda

*B*renda Barnes was 5' 5" tall, with brown skin, clear eyes and enormous bright Tiffany chandelier-like teeth. Her parents were friendly neighbors and sometimes my family and her family attended Heritage Baptist Church together. Brenda was always a great test taker with natural confidence. When called upon to read or give a presentation in front of a class Brenda's spirit shined. She really came into her own in middle school when she was selected to sing a few solos for the church choir and become our 8th grade class president and class valedictorian. But every rose has a few thorns. Brenda was a notoriously nosy blabber mouth who enjoyed seeing anyone she deemed a threat, become embarrassed or just plain fail. In 8th grade there were plenty of smart students that could have been class president like Stacey Newton and Hubert Crawford. When kindhearted Stacy became too popular, someone decided to pour melted cheese whiz all over her unattended solar system models just before her Science Fair presentation. Stacy had a nervous breakdown. When Hubert became a top prospect, someone spread rumors that he made out with a carousel horse at the shopping mall causing him to admit that he collected miniature porcelain animals and cry uncontrollably in front of his football teammates. Poor Hubert never recovered! That 'someone' was never officially caught or named, but I knew. Most kids knew. If Brenda wanted something and you were in her way, she simply pushed you into the volcano without warning or concern for Kantian ethics. Brenda was also part of a click that called itself 'The God Sisters' with big boobed Shonelle, Tina, and Georgette that started way back in 5th grade. Any of those chicks in Brenda's click would take a bullet for her. Brenda was smart, popular, and ruthless. No one wants to be an adversary to that!

As Knowledge finished the last of his chocolate milk and threw away his carrots and tray, he literally bumped into an old nemesis,

Chauncey "Dragon" Fogle. Dragon was the kid who beat Knowledge Born to a pulp in Carver Park a few years ago because Knowledge tried to prevent his friend's bike from being stolen by Dragon's crew of creeps. He was later expelled from Knowledge's old school soon after that incident for breaking a teacher's jaw. I never saw him until now. The bumping into Knowledge was no accident. Dragon didn't even belong in the café at that time. He was already a sophomore at Northside and wanted to jumpstart big time trouble with Knowledge whose own rep grew spectacularly since their earlier confrontation. Knowledge was now taller and stronger; both physically and instinctually. I knew Knowledge wanted revenge, but now wasn't the time. It was the first day of high school for us and Knowledge knew to be cool.

"(Humph). What's up, Kevin," spoke Dragon with head leaning sideways, smirking through his toothpick chewing.

"Kevin is my slave name; a name that doesn't capture my true station in life. My name is now Knowledge Born."

"(Humph). So you're some serious religious dude now or something, huh? (Humph). That don't mean nothing to me. You stay in your place and you just might survive the day, FAT boy."

"My place...as you put it is where ever God wants me. And as far as surviving the day...I will survive every day of my life with the wisdom of a thousand elephants and the strength of a thousand bears."

"(Humph). More like the strength of a thousand jellyfishes, FAT boy. Hahaaa!"

"Actually, a jellyfish, despite an unusual name and an awkward appearance, is capable of giving an unpleasant sting."

"Oh, (Humph).Well, I guess I'll see you A-Round then, FAT boy. (Humph)."

"I guess so."

I was proud of Knowledge for not flinching. He was new to high school, but not new to life. He'd been through way more trials and tribulations than me up to that point. Come what may, he seemed ready! I, on the other hand, was as green as spinach and saw high school as a brand new planet. I was afraid of what Dragon might pull and I didn't have the foggiest idea as to what the future might hold.

"Hey, Breezy. Read Chapter 1 and do questions 1, 2, 4, 5, and 7 on pages 34 and 35."

"Thanks, Knowledge Born. Who was that tall kid you were talking to," asked nosy 'Big Mouth' Brenda.

"He's nobody, really," said Knowledge calmly. And with that, Knowledge and I grabbed our shiny book bags and left the cafeteria for our 7th period classes. I had Algebra I with Mr. Quilinski who enjoyed being called Mr. Q.

Mr. Q was in his late 40's, had perfectly cropped salt-&-pepper hair and always wore a white shirt and tie. He was the neatest person I ever saw. His desk was always immaculate. His clothes had that dry cleaned look. His shoes shined like blown glass fresh from the fire. Even his handwriting looked like he typesetted the words onto the chalkboard! Mr. Q was a no-nonsense, don't-you-dare-ask-me-anything-stupid kind of teacher. He did the talking; you listened. Students rarely stepped out of line in his presence or challenged his authority.

"Good afternoon, class. Welcome to Algebra I. My name is Mr. Q. I know it's been a long day, but please bear with me for a moment. I just want to make sure that everyone who is here, should be in this class. I am passing around an attendance sheet in which I would like everyone to put their full name, along with an emergency telephone number where your parents can be reached just in case such a situation should arise. Now... by a show of hands, how many of you love algebra?"

Only two hands went up; one of which was mine. Mr. Q quickly pointed in my direction and calmly asked me what I knew about algebra and I stated a few basic facts about how coordinate systems have two number lines, one horizontal and one vertical and they are great for displaying pairs of numbers; how a real number is any given distance from a zero to any point on the number line; and how the square root of a given number equals a non-negative number that, when squared equal the original given number. Mr. Q seemed surprised to hear anything that remotely resembled algebra from a freshman. He was also delighted and politely nodded when I told him my shop major was electronics. Mr. Q said he and Mr. Torello were old friends. It was my best moment of the day.

Algebra class, for me at least, went by as fast and smoothly as an albatross sailing through the air on a warm clear morning. The notes that we took in class were just review points for me, no biggie. -- 8th and 9th periods were strictly reserved for the freshmen's shop classes. There was Printing, Welding, Cosmetology, Construction, Nursing, Drafting, Commercial Art, Business, Auto Body, Refrigeration, Engine Mechanics, Culinary Arts, and Electronics. While applying to Northside, every student had to already know what they want to be and select a shop major. After being accepted, each freshman had only three weeks to change their minds and make a new selection.

RIINNNGGGG!!

After walking the long hallway to the Electronics classroom I looked for Knowledge, but of course he was late and sat in the back. I took my sit further up front to make a good impression and Mr. Torello wasted no time in jolting everyone's circulatory system with his booming voice. When he spoke, he never looked at anyone directly; he spoke as if he was on a Broadway stage, playing King Creon in "Antigone". My first day in shop class was as long as the Old Testament, with Mr. Torello giving us every intellectual nook and cranny he could muster on some of the key founding fathers and history of electronics. We learned about people such as William Crookes, Karl Ferdinand Braun and Guglielmo Marconi; we learned about cathode rays, the discovery of the electron and vacuum tubes. Mr. Torello seemed to love electronics the way Beethoven loved the piano. He talked the whole two periods, nonstop without taking a breath. We were all mentally and spiritually drained. Our brains simply couldn't absorb any more information about electrons or waves. I think Mr. Torello's idea was to chase away any student who thought electronics would be easy just because they took apart and reassembled their mother's toaster; to chase away students who were just pretenders and not principled. That

afternoon seven students changed their shop major from electronics to anything else that was available. They just couldn't take it. I thought Mr. Torello's strategy was brilliant.

RIINNNGGGG!!

Finally, the final school bell rang and we were all temporarily emancipated. My first day of high school was over and I was grateful too still be alive.

"That was intense, huh G-man," Knowledge said as we both tried to escape amongst the chaos and hysteria that was unfolding in the hallways.

"Yep," I said, thinking Knowledge was referring to Mr. Torello's verbal head crusher.

"I've got to demolish that sucker Dragon", Knowledge said furiously.

"Well, I think..."

"I ain't gonna let that fool chump me at Northside, ya heard G-man! Things are different now! I live by a new creed. If that sucker wants to start up, I'm ready for him and anybody who's down with him! I ain't havin' none of that! The past is in the past as far as I'm concerned and I wannabe a righteous black man, but I'm NOT gettin' chumped here or anywhere else- word up!!"

"Yep."

"I'm serious G-man. I gotta do something to Dragon before he starts gathering up steam."

"I hear you loud and clear. What's the plan?"

"I'm not sure yet, but I need to know if I can count on you G-man."

Me? Me??!! What the heck do I have to do with Knowledge's personal beef with Dragon? I wasn't even there when Dragon's crew jumped Knowledge. Dragon didn't even know who I was and I wanted it to stay that way. I definitely didn't want to get in the middle of power struggle between a tornado and a hurricane. I didn't want to get in the middle of anything – not one thing.

"Sure bro", I said.

"Bet."

Maybe it was moral support Knowledge was talking about and needed- I could surely do that, I thought. However, hand-to-hand combat is out of the question! Knowledge must know I'm not a battleship. Knowledge's future revenge plans made me more nervous than a one-legged man going skydiving. Whatever he was going to cook up would be cold and bold, that I knew for sure. -- Maybe I could be conveniently sick on Knowledge's day of bringing back the Spanish Inquisition. I wanted no part of carnage.

"G-man, I got a ride with this senior named Brother Star. Wanna roll with us', asked Knowledge- his voice much calmer, 'he should be here any minute now. He's never late."

"No, bro. I'll hike it."

"Alright G-man. Later. - Don't forget about hanging at Captain Sam's Arcade on Saturday. You promised you'd hang at 12noon to play Pac-Man and shoot some at the hoops machine. Remember?"

"I didn't forget. I'll be there."

"Bet."

Just before school started Knowledge wanted us to go back to Captain Sam's again. I think he wanted to regain some of his pride back. We played seven games of 8-ball last time and each time I crushed the life out of him. Knowledge was a thick athletic kid with heavy hands and because of that he thought he could beat me at anything. He was always treated as if he was older than he really was and that made him a target. Some of the older kids liked him because they thought of him as an equal and some guys were jealous of that. Kids always wanted Knowledge on their team in gym class and teachers always used him to run errands for them like carrying books from the supply room and such. We became friends during Summer Camp at Heritage Baptist Church a few summers ago. I think he felt he could trust me because I was quieter than most and

I didn't care for the gossip that ran rampant in church and school. Truth be told, Knowledge was an ordinary scared crap-less kid who was just trying to make his way in this lopsided, hypocritical world and so was I.

Wednesday was a repeat of Tuesday with three exceptions. The first was I finally got a chance to meet my first period teacher for Sociology, Mrs. Ball. She showed us the first forty minutes of the film 'The Verdict' starring Paul Newman and told the class, if we wanted to see the rest of the film, we could during her afterschool program. All of the students did just that. The movie was intense and gripping. The only other movie I ever saw Paul Newman in was 'The Hustler' and that is my favorite film of all time. The second was I read and memorized a passage from the bible during my cafeteria time. It is the following...

I pray that out of his glorious riches he may strengthen you with power through his Spirit in your inner being, so that Christ may dwell in your hearts through faith. And I pray that you, being rooted and established in love, may have power, together with all the saints, to grasp how wide and long and high and deep is the love of Christ, and to know this love that surpasses knowledge-that you may be filled to the measure of all the fullness of God. Now to him who is able to do immeasurably more than all we ask or imagine, according to his power that is at work within us, to him be glory in the church and in Christ Jesus throughout all generations, for ever and ever! Amen (Ephesians 3:16-21).

The third was Jennifer Gooden wore a fancy blue blouse and matching skirt.

Chapter 6

Colored Marbles

*T*hursday was only the third day into our freshman year, the Thursday after Labor Day, and I knew that my first couple of days in high school were going to be filled with more engaging hippie insight on Western Civilization, more writing assignments in English Composition (I'm still waiting for Mrs. Slate to grade and return my 'Hero' paper), more scientific jargon and talk of colored marbles, folders and jars in Science class, more instruction on how to approach a volleyball, more quizzes in Algebra and more clarification on facts concerning the forefathers of electronics.

The first week of school is always for the teachers to get their engines revved up again after a summer spent sleeping late in beach houses, going on weight loss programs, writing screenplays or working in their vegetable gardens. The first week was also for us freshmen to get used to the fast lane of learning that is high school. However, all I could think about was Saturday at Captain Sam's Arcade. What was the plan to take down Dragon? That Thursday I knew Dragon and his crew started with Knowledge again in the morning, calling him all kinds of names and even threating to bring a gun to school to finish Knowledge off. Knowledge was getting angrier, but refused help from his newer friends like Supreme Justice, Brother Star, and Universal who wanted to step in and break Dragon's snout and rip off his wings. -- Knowledge's step-father was a corrections officer and, in Knowledge's mind at least, respect had to be achieved without doing something so serious as to getting himself expelled or ending up in a detention faculty. His step-father would have flipped if that had happened. Knowledge had to fight with his own tactics. He told the 'brothers' he had a plan and was playing his cards close to his vest. 'The brothers' trusted Knowledge's wisdom but were monitoring the situation closely. If Knowledge couldn't handle his problem in a time efficient manner, it would have looked bad on all of them and Knowledge's quest for an upwardly mobile rep would be finished. Everybody waited.

I had just finished taking Mr. Connelly's first Thursday test which was all multiple choice and he said I did very well and could leave a little early for my next class. The day was moving in a positive direction when...

"Hi, Bagel Boy. What's new in the world of the clueless and pathetic?"

"Good news, Brenda. I hear the FDA is only a few weeks away from approving an over the counter drug that cures demonic possession. Excited?"

"I am saved, Bagel Boy. Praise the Lord, Hallelujah," Brenda said smirking and rolling her bright eyes.

"Church folk. (Whew). I tell you, some of them never declare a word of encouragement or edification. Can I get an Amen?"

Brenda laughed genuinely through firmly sealed lips and lightly punched the upper part of my shoulder as we both walked together to Mrs. Slate's Literature class.

"Did you read Chapter 1, Acts 1-4 in Macbeth, Bagel Boy? I hope Mrs. Slate's quizzes are multiple choices."

"Yeah. I think she said there's only going to be ten questions. I hope we finally get our 'Hero' papers back today."

"True that. Who do you have for first period?"

"I have Mrs. Ball for Sociology. All she does is show us movies and the students talk about the main idea, the film's impact on society, stuff like that. I think she said she's been teaching for 38 years."

"So you get to play Siskel and Ebert, huh Bagel Boy? That sounds like fun. What movies have you watched so far?"

"She showed us the 'The Verdict' with Paul Newman which is pretty awesome. It's about a down-on-his-luck lawyer who takes on a case where the odds are nearly insurmountable. It's intense and very realistic."

"Cool. I'm going to have to catch that one sometime."

We walked in quietly into class. Mrs. Slate was on her classroom phone jibber-jabbering away.

"ALL he does is push that STUPID shopping cart of HIS AROUND...I know, right...YEAH. HE'S a TOTAL moron!! He's one step from it, THAT'S FOR SURE!! I know, RIGHT...After his divorce that man lost his MARBLES ALRIGHT...HEEEEEHAHAHAAHAHAAAA!!!!!"

As the seconds rolled away and more students poured into the class we could see Mrs. Slate swivel her chair, reach inside her binder and plop the 'Hero' papers down on the corner of her desk. Somebody had a big fat red D- on the top of their paper.

"Boy-o-boy, I hope that's not my paper," I thought quietly.

"Ok, BABE. See you in the CAFÉ," said Mrs. Slate as she finally hung up her beat up beige lipstick stained class phone.

"Well, NOW! I've graded your 'Hero' papers...and some were nicely written...and SOME were...how can I put this...total GAR-BAGE!! Brenda, please pass THESE out. Thank you, hon. -- I've recorded your grades in my GRADE book. If anyone THINKS they can do a make-up paper, well, TOUGH NOODLES! I NEVER allow make-ups unless there's a SERIOUS medical issue involved. OTHERWISE, all grades in MY CLASS are FINAL. So there."

Oh, no. Brenda is going to see my 'Hero' paper grade before me. I hope I at least got a B. As I looked around the room, every-body seemed to have their paper to either smile at or hide from, except for me. In my peripheral vision I could see Brenda marching toward me from my left. I quickly glanced at her to read her facial expression. My paper was last and Brenda poker-faced me.

"An A-? Hooray," I said proudly.

"I got an A+, Bagel Boy," Brenda whispered in my ear. She slowly strutted back to her seat and sneakily stuck out her tongue in my direction.

"Darn it," I thought. "I wanted Brenda's rein to cease. I wanted Brenda's little suck up paper to be burned. I wanted Brenda to be arrested and jailed for flying without a broom permit. I wanted..."

"Okay, NOW...everyone PASS your 'Hero' papers FORWARD so I can keep them on FILE. Also TAKE out a PIECE of paper SO that WE can begin our quiz on MACBETH," shouted Mrs. Slate. "NOW, that everyone has READ Act 1, SCENES 1-4,' Mrs. Slate rubbed her two palms together as if to start a fire, 'we can BEGIN!"

Everybody was scrambling for a half loose leaf paper and jotting down Mrs. Slate's special heading which she deducted points, if not written to match her exact specifications.

"In MACBETH, WHO is the KING of SCOTLAND?"

I quickly wrote my heading and numbered my half paper vertically 1 through 10, skipping a line all the way down and wrote

'Duncan' next to number 1. I could feel the butterflies arm wrestling in my gut.

"NAME the TWO Scottish GENERALS that FOUGHT with GREAT courage?"

Hmmm. I knew for sure one was Macbeth...and the other was... Banquo...I was 90% sure on that one.

Mrs. Slate yelled eight more questions and I was able to answer all of them. As to whether they were all right was another matter. The poor chubby kid to my left only answered about five. Even if he got all five right he would still fail the quiz. All that chubby kid ever talked about and wanted to be in life was a baker. That's why he arrived at Northside. He couldn't care less about Macbeth or anything else for that matter, it was written all over him. As Shakespeare put it, "Fair is foul, and foul is fair."

My day was going by so fast that I'd forgotten all about Knowledge's beef with Dragon. I felt good about my earlier test in West Civilization, my first quiz on Macbeth and was sort of happy about my A-. I guess the two spelling errors on "extraordinary" and "previously" cost me a few points. Brenda wrote nearly two full pages on Pastor McDonaldson, her experiences in church and summer camp and probably didn't misspell a single word. Brenda was definitely smart. No one was denying her proper credit. I just wanted...

RIINNNGGGG!!

That was the end of 3rd period and everyone scattered to their next torture chamber.

"Just remember students, 'Smile and the world will smile with you,'" said our principal Mrs. Brunswick for the umpteenth time as she walked down the hallway with her brick-sized walkie-talkie and clipboard. I couldn't understand why she chose that particular saying to run with. It had nothing to do with educational excellence, trying one's best, or perseverance. It just struck me as a very arbitrary thing to say to young people. But then again, life itself was sort of an arbitrary event. I could have been born a different color in a different time in a different place with different parents. Or not born at all. Why did God create all these different races, nationalities, languages anyway? Why were there so many wars? Couldn't there have been a more simple recipe to all this? What was our purpose? Mrs. Brunswick believed that our purpose in life was to smile. No matter who they were, where or when...no matter the circumstances, just smile. At least she had an answer. I didn't.

As I strolled to Mr. Bassford's class, which was the longest forty minute block anybody has ever heard of, my head was totally in the clouds. The hallway noises and madness seemed melodic. Miles Davis was playing "Sketches of Spain" on a trumpet in the background. I was surrounded by long-legged beautiful women dressed as billiard balls dancing on floating green felt and I was an all-powerful king holding a golden cue stick as my sceptre. -- Daydreaming was the life raff that kept me from drowning at Northside.

When I walked into Mr. Bassford's Science class, I grabbed my yellow folder from the yellow bin located at the window sill marked '4th Period' and sat at the yellow table and waited patiently for the opportunity to earn a yellow marble placed in the jar with the yellow label also marked '4th Period'. Mr. Bassford was late again. Students were throwing papers across the room, talking loudly, seating on top of desks, and some goofy looking kid was even making out with his girlfriend in the lab area- a place where no one was allowed unless told otherwise.

"Good morning. Please take your proper seats where you've been assigned. Please stop talking. And whoever that is in the lab area – if you're not one of my students during this time period please leave now. Thank you. I appreciate it. I'll wait."

"Hey, Mr. Bassford, bite me," the goofy looking kid yelled as he and his laughing girlfriend exited the rear science lab door.

Mr. Bassford stood in front of the classroom as calm as a statue with hands folded behind his back not saying a single word. His left eye was switching like crazy. Students began lowering their noise level and suddenly an eerie silence hovered over the classroom. For about ten long seconds my fellow classmates and I thought we might need to dive under our tables for cover.

"Thank you class. I appreciate that. (sigh) Okay. Today we will discuss and learn about magnets. How they attract and repel different metals. Do they influence other things besides metals? Can, let's say, magnets have an effect on the growth of a plant," Mr. Bassford let out an even heavier sigh and continued. "We will also discuss and learn about light. How it affects food, bread, ants, etc.

I have matching colored handout sheets for everyone that directly correlates with your colored folders. Make sure after we conduct our experiments and write down our conclusions you place your specific colored handouts in your specific colored folders. I appreciate that. Thank you. And after we're done today, I will see which colored group receives a shiny brand new colored marble... I don't know if I mentioned it to this class or not already, but I used to love playing with marbles when was a child..."

When I looked up at the wall to check the time it was as if Salvador Dali had melted the clock still. 32 more minutes in Mr. Bassford's class was going to be an agonizing eternity. There also seemed to be an unspoken consensus amongst the students that not a single person would dare ask any questions in his class. No one, I guess, wanted to be a stand out or be in Mr. Bassford's crosshairs. My colored group didn't even win a marble today either. Darn.

Chapter 7

Decisions

*A*fter Science, I was so drained I didn't think I had the strength to do any jumping jacks, climb a rope or whatever Ms. Gomez had in store for us. I was ready for a one round fight – my head hitting the pillow and the pillow knocking me out.

As I walked toward the gymnasium I started daydreaming again. -- I was brought into an enormous courtroom by guards with gigantic 9-ball heads. I was being charged with pool player treason. The judge said I broke my oath to play pool every day. They dragged me in front of a firing squad of soldiers that all looked like Brenda! They all took aim and...

"Yo, G-man. I've got to talk you for a minute before we get to gym class."

"Sure. What's going on?"

"This Friday, do you think you can teach me how to shoot pool? You know, like really good…like you…"

"Ummm…I, I really don't know…"

"Yo, I'm super serious G-man. I found out that that punk Dragon is a small time shark at Raul's Pool Hall on Route 13, not too far from, you know, that big gas station over there. Do you know the place I'm talking about? Dragon and his boys always ride their bikes up and hang out there. Brother Star told me that Dragon likes to hustle fools at 9-ball for like ten bucks a rack and has never lost. I've never heard of 9-ball, have you ever played it before?"

"Yeah. I've played 9-ball before. But, I…"

"Good. So it's settled then. You teach me some of that 9-ball trick stuff and in about an hour I'll be ready for my battle at Raul's. Thanks G-man!! I knew I could count on you. Peace be upon you."

"Wait a sec…"

Knowledge left before I could think straight or utter a complete thought. He was already wearing his sweatpants and sneakers, so I couldn't even explain to him in the locker room that no one can master 9-ball in an hour, much less someone like him. I've played 8-ball against Knowledge at the arcade before and he couldn't even make his straight in shots with the object ball hanging in the pocket! Did Knowledge already talk himself into a pool challenge at Raul's against a street thug like Dragon? This was his plan for revenge? Was there money involved? If so, Knowledge was walking straight into a booby trap. Friday was also my dad's birthday. My mom had the cake and presents all set. Because my dad always worked long hours, seven days a week, celebrating birthdays and holidays were especially important in my family. How was I going to teach 9-ball to Knowledge at Captain Sam's which was all the way downtown and wish my dad a happy birthday at the same time? I was definitely not daydreaming now.

I quickly ran into the locker room and threw on my favorite blue shorts and stuffed my backpack with my pants and shirt because I didn't have my combination lock yet. -- Ms. Gomez didn't seem to care that I was a little late and told all her students to line up on the black line and do stretching exercises. I asked Jennifer Gooden, the cute girl from my Western Civilization class, to watch my backpack for me. She wanted to look over her nursing books on the bleachers and elected to skip gym. -- My mind was racing in a thousand directions.

After we rotated our arms and necks and touched our toes, I really wasn't in any mood for volleyball. I glanced over at the other side of the gym and Knowledge was as carefree and unenlightened as any of the chained captives facing the blank wall in Plato's "Allegory of the Cave." I was the one worrying. I was the one who knew the truth. And I was the one who had to set things straight.

"Remember class, front row blocks and hits, back row plays defense. Okay? 'I will try' on the count of three, 1 – 2 – 3..."

"I WILL TRY!!!!!"

"Also don't forget class...," continued Ms. Gomez. "You're either passing, setting or hitting back that high ball. Okay?"

"I WILL TRY," shouted the class.

Most of us had no clue as to what we were doing. Some kids were hitting the ball too hard. Some kids couldn't serve properly. Some kids were tripping over each other. No one knew which team was winning or losing. It was organized chaos unleashed. It was total fun and I had a blast!

RIINNNGGGG!!

It was now the end of 5th period, which meant I had only a few minutes to change back into my regular clothes and head to the cafeteria.

"Thanks a bunch Jennifer," I said.

"You're welcome Grice."

I looked to see if I saw Knowledge anywhere around, but he was already gone as if he evaporated or something. No biggie I thought. I'll catch him at lunch. I threw my pants on over my shorts and put my newly wrinkled shirt back on and walked as fast as I could to the café. I didn't want Mrs. Brunswick to yell at me for running.

When I arrived at the cafeteria it was a complete madhouse and all the groups had already marked off their territories. Athletic kids, preppy kids, wannabes, flunkies, squares, popular girls, average girls, counter-culturists, clowns all had their spots. I quietly took my tray of a spoonful of baked beans, a single hotdog, a cup of apple sauce and a carton of milk and sat with the nobodies. They were doing your mama' jokes.

"Your mother is so stupid, she spelled 'cat' with a number," said the first kid.

"Oooo," two kids shouted.

"Your mother is so fat, she can't fit on a beach," said a second kid.

"Oh SNAP," yelled another.

"Your mother is so ugly, she made a grown man cry," said the first kid.

"Ooooooooooo," the whole table was shaking and laughing, except for me. Where was Knowledge? I had a ton to get off my chest. Maybe he was somewhere talking to 'the brothers', going over their strategy for taking down Dragon. -- I was surrounded by the volcanic energy of noisy kids and still I felt alone.

I ate my dog and apple sauce as fast as I could and drank only half my milk. I looked around to see if I saw Brenda. She was yak-king away with Georgette and some other girls in the corner. I guess that's where the top gun broom pilots sit, I thought quietly.

"Hi, Grice. Do you mind if I sit here," asked Jennifer Gooden, dressed in a fancy purple blouse with a matching skirt. She looked like a girl born of royalty.

"Sure."

"What did you get on Mr. Connelly's quiz," asked Jennifer Gooden as she slowly scooped her slightly frozen apple sauce with her spork.

"He just said, 'I did well,' and that was all."

"Same here. I like Mr. Connelly, he seems cool. -- You looked like you loved playing volleyball back there in gym class. That boy with the 'E.T' shirt was wrong to smack the ball into your face like that. I thought you were going to smack him back."

"I'm not sweating that. If that dude is proud to wear a played out 'E.T. Phone Home' shirt in public, he's already smacked himself, you know what I mean?"

"That's so true. You're funny, Grice," laughed Jennifer Gooden.

"E.T.? C'mon. That movie came out, what, like three years ago, right? He must think that movie is a documentary or something. That dude...he probably hopes a U.F.O. lands in his underpants."

Jennifer Gooden laughed genuinely and then smiled. She had a nice laugh. < Our eyes locked for a split second. >

"Yo, G-man. Where you been hiding," interrupted Knowledge as he walked over and stood over us.

"I'll see you later, Grice. It was nice chatting with you," said Jennifer Gooden as she stood up, grabbed her books, politely waved back at me and walked out of the café. I could have strangled Knowledge right there.

"Who's tttthat,"asked Knowledge checking out my Jennifer Gooden as she walked away. "You trying to get with that, G-man? I hear ya! She's a little flat though..."

"I can't teach you 9-ball in an hour and besides my dad's birthday is Friday so I can't hang, I repeat I can't hang at Sam's on that day! Did you hear me? Do I need a megaphone? Or is there cotton in your ears?!!"

"Whoa. What's up with all that, G-man?"

"Nothing's up! I just can't...I understand your situation and I want to help out...but, I just can't do anything on Friday, ok?"

"Ok, man. – We're gonna have to talk to 'the brothers' about this, you know that right? They thought our plan was all set. There's serious money involved in this thing. So, I'm gonna need you to go to Carver Park with me today, just...only for a few minutes, just to square things up and hash out a different strategy. Ok, G-man? Just give me that much..."

"What's this 'we' stuff?"

"I told 'the brothers' that you were a cool Christian dude that knows how to shoot pool, would be glad to be a part of our hustle and that you would never sell out a friend. So, G-man – what's it going to be?! Can I count on YOU or what?"

"Eh, alright."

Chapter 8

Electronics

*A*nd with that said, I calmly threw away my tray and slowly walked from the cafeteria. Knowledge trailed along, but there weren't any more words between us as we entered shop. Mr. Torello was standing at full attention, notes in hand and ready to bark. His head was gleaming like a brand new cue ball, I thought quietly.

Shop class went by as slow as an old snail trying to do the Cha-cha slide. Mr. Torello could talk for days, but I took notes that barely resembled the English language. All I could think about was pool and my heart pounded loudly at the thought of seeing any type of real shootout involving a young pool hustler. Was Dragon really that good? Mr. Evans could beat him, I'd bet. I wondered if I could.

Dragon was a tall, skinny, tough-looking acerbic light-skin kid that was almost 18 years-old and just beginning his sophomore year at Northside. He majored in construction but rarely attended class. He had long arms and a noticeable scar above the left side of his upper lip. He had already been in a juvenile detention faculty for narcotics and gun possession. Everyone knew he was evidentially going to prison; it was written in his eyes. There was sadness to Dragon, the way he walked and talked, that made him seem more dangerous, like being alive was some sort of a burden. Nothing seemed to matter to him. He wanted to go to prison, I guess. Dragon seemed to be a kid who never understood or was never taught the true meaning of *agape*. Without it no one is complete. Thinking about Dragon made me search my own inner being. Whatever Dragon's deal was, I was surprised to find out that he was a good pool player. Maybe he practices when he cuts classes. I cringed at the thought of thinking I had something in common with Dragon. Rumor was that he was the love child of a married Italian mobster and his black mother was a prostitute. Dragon's maternal grandmother tried her best to raise him with morals, but there is only so much a single elderly woman can do. Perhaps his anger at the world stemmed from that. I truly didn't know. All I knew was that Dragon intimidated nearly every kid he encountered and I was glad and a little jealous, that it was Knowledge going up against this dude and not me.

RIINNNGGGG!!

The final school bell of the day is one of the sweetest sounds known to man. It's right up there with the laughter of children at play. Freedom is the water of life. I waited patiently outside Mr. Torello's classroom for Knowledge.

"Yo, G-man, I don't want you to be afraid of these 'brothers,' alright," said Knowledge as we walked down the hallway toward the exit.

"I know."

"Brother Star's got a car and he'll meet us by the students' parking lot, alright?"

"Ok."

"The Five Percent Nation believes and teaches that black people are the true original people of this planet; that black people are the fathers and mothers of civilization; and that the black man is God."

"Yeah."

"As a rule we Five-percenters are forbidden to eat pork or any pork-based by-products, alright? I hope you didn't eat that hotdog from the cafe. That's why I skipped lunch today. Hotdogs, sausages, bacon are evil, bro."

"Alright."

"So, whatever you do, tell 'the brothers' that you don't eat swine of any kind, alright?"

"Ok."

"Do you have any questions before we meet 'the brothers'?"

"Who started the 5% Nation?"

"A teacher named Clarence 13X, who was once a part of the Nation of Islam started the philosophy of 5% Nation. We're also known as The Nation of Gods and Earths, alright?"

"Ok."

Knowledge and I continued walking and talking.

BEEP! BEEP!

"That's Brother Star, G-man. Let's go."

"Ok."

Brother Star was an honor roll student with a good personality and a senior at Northside. He had been in a few fistfights, but otherwise was highly respected among fellow students and teachers alike. He majored in cosmetology so he could become a licensed barber and own his own barbershop like his uncle. He already had experience cutting heads in his grandmother's basement and was smart with his money. He also had spotless brown skin due to the fact that he was a vegetarian and kept himself in shape. Girls of all shades liked and responded well to him. Brother Star was only 5'8" but seemed much taller and more mature than most kids his age. He had uncommon integrity and was a great ambassador of his beliefs.

"As-salaam alaikum, young bloods," said Brother Star as he drove up in his '78 Chevy Nova and unhooked the passenger side lock. Run-D.M.C.'s "It's Like That" thumped on the car's cassette player.

"Alaikum Salaam," replied Knowledge proudly. "This is G-man."

I crawled into the back seat and Knowledge sat in the front passenger seat.

"Yeah, I can see that young blood. What's your government name?"

"My name is Grafton. Grice Grafton."

"Ok, James Bond. It's always a pleasure to meet intelligent young brothers. – So, young blood, what's going on," asked Brother Star talking to Knowledge.

"We need to change the plans on Dragon. My main man, G-man, right here can't teach me 9-ball in time for our set-up on Saturday."

"Keep talking young blood, I'm listening," said Brother Star as pulled out of Northside's parking lot and waved at a tall pretty girl who shouted, "Bye Star!"

"I have a confession to make. I, I can't play pool as well as I said I could before, Brother Star,' said Knowledge, 'I didn't mean to mislead you or 'the brothers'. The fact is I can't play at all. But my man, G-man has serious skills. He's really good!! I've seen his game at Captain Sam's Arcade. He tore it up on that pool table! He should play Dragon, word up!!" I was stunned and silent.

"First and foremost, I want to thank you young blood for speaking the truth just now. The whole point of 5% Nation is that all the people who know the truth, speak the truth. You're definitely growing in your wisdom which is allowing you to become a man. All praise to Allah." Before we went to Carver Park, Brother Star stopped at the barber shop for about 20 minutes so he could talk to his uncle. Knowledge and I sat quietly in the car and listened to Whodini's "Friends", Pumpkin's "King of the Beat", Run-DMC's "Hard Times", and Fearless Four's "Problems of the World Today." When Brother Star returned he continued talking as Grandmaster Flash and the Furious Five's "The Message" earthquaked on cassette. I could barely hear him above the music.

"Now, young blood,' said Brother Star looking at me through the rear view mirror, 'can you really play 9-ball? I mean really play because Dragon ain't a joke with a pool stick and there's two-hundred U.S. dollars riding on this thing. You're not obligated in any way. This is Knowledge's test, not yours. I can easily cancel our appointment for Saturday at Raul's and set something else up. Understand?"

"Yeah. Count me in." Brother Star took his sunglasses off, turned the music off, parked and turned his body around to look squarely into my face. Knowledge looked straight ahead and was quiet.

"Are you sure, young blood? Don't let your friendship with Knowledge Born pressure your decision. If you don't want to do it, say so now. There won't be any hard feelings. You don't owe any-body here anything and I'll make sure that Knowledge Born doesn't give you any problems later. My word is my bond. Understand?"

"I understand. Deal me in."

"Ok, young blood. You've got heart; that much I can see,' Brother Star then turned back to Knowledge and whispered, 'If your man doesn't win, you're gonna owe the two-hundred plus interest. Understand?"

"Yes, Brother Star," replied Knowledge. We all got out of the Chevy Nova and walked toward the upper portion of Carver Park just opposite the playground. The tall monument of General George Washington crossing the Delaware River at the Battle of Trenton on Christmas night during the American Revolution in 1776 was 'the brothers' favorite spot to debate, listen to music, play chess or workout. There was also a group of Puerto-Rican break dancers that Thursday afternoon displaying their acrobatic skills near the monument. They called themselves "The Dynamite Breaker's Crew." They were incredible.

Supreme Justice and Universal were already there in solid b-boy gear standing on the curb next to a well-dressed gentleman wearing a bow-tie sitting inside a new 1984 Ford Thunderbird re-listening to a cassette of Minister Farrakhan's first Saviour's Day speech delivered back in 1981 in Chicago. The car was white and black two-tone with a red pinstripe on the sides. That was the car I wanted to drive when I got older, I thought quietly.

It was early September and Carver Park was still filled with the youthful energy of summer. Kids were playing basketball. Kids were on the swings. Kids were showing off new clothes and flirting. It was a great time to be young and alive.

"Ok, young blood,' Brother Star said looking at me, 'I want you to meet 'the brothers.' Knowledge Born, you'll be the one to introduce him. Understand?"

"Alright," said Knowledge. As we walked over to meet the rest of the posse, I could feel my chest tighten.

"As-salaam alaikum," said Knowledge and Brother Star.

"Alaikum salaam," Supreme Justice and Universal replied in unison. 'Brotherly' handshakes followed.

"This guy right here... is a good brother; we go way back from our days at Heritage Baptist Church Summer Camp. Right, G-man? His government name is Grice, but I always call him G-man."

"What's up, Grice," spoke Universal.

"It's a pleasure to meet you guys," I said calmly.

"Alright, alright. So, how you like it at Northside so far,' asked Universal.

"It's cool," I said.

"Grice is going play Dragon on Saturday on account he's a better fit for a win. Understand," said Brother Star.

"Alright, alright. So you been shootin' some pool in your days, huh?"

"Yeah."

"Alright. I can dig it. You better win, too, brother. I got some of my money tied up in this game."

"I will try," I said repeating Ms. Gomez's inspirational chant.

"Hi, Bagel Boy," yelled 'Big Mouth' Brenda from the playground.

She was with Shonelle and Georgette. I tried to ignore her.

"What's the matter Bagel Boy, you can't speak," Brenda said walking closer to 'the brothers'. I wanted to crawl into a hole and die. Knowledge had a smirk on his face.

"Hello, sisters. I want to give you a complimentary copy of 'The Final Call'. We as a people, especially the young ones, need to come together to keep the strong black family going strong," said the gentleman in the bow-tie. Brenda smiled, took the newspaper and said "Thank you."

"Hello, young Nubian queens. You ladies look more and more beautiful each day," said Supreme Justice.

"Hello, sisters," said Universal.

"Hey, Breezy," said Knowledge.

"How are you, Brenda? Where are you and your friends headed," asked Brother Star.

"Oh, hi. Hi, Brenda," I said.

"Hi, gentlemen. Hi, Star. – 'Oh, hi' my foot, Bagel Boy. Don't start acting funny just because you're surrounded by MY cousin and HIS friends. I'll bet you didn't even know that Star is my second cousin."

"What happened, Brenda? Did you crash your broom again," I said sharply.

"I hope you intelligent, strong, courageous black men can talk some sense into Bagel Boy. He needs real guidance." Shonelle and Georgette giggled in the background. 'The brothers' stood with their arms folded in a b-boy stance not saying a word. The gentleman in the bow-tie adjusted his car radio. And Knowledge was still smirking.

"Wait a minute, Brenda. Slow it down. Why do you call this young blood, 'Bagel Boy'? His name is Grice. Show some respect," said Brother Star.

"All he eats are those nasty bagels in the morning. Every day, and I mean every day, we used to walk to school with the twins he would go to Angie's grocery store and buy a cinnamon raisin bagel with butter. Isn't that true, Bagel Boy?"

"Wait a minute, Brenda. Hold your horses. We're over here discussing pertinent business, so you and your little crew need to run along. Understand? Tell your mom that Nana's 80th birthday party will be on Sunday inside the church, not Saturday. Pastor

McDonaldson and his wife have something special planned for her during and after service."

"Ok, Star. See you gentlemen later. Oh, bye Bagel Boy. – Let's go, girls."

"What was all that about, Grice," asked a perplexed Universal looking at me then Brother Star.

"Brenda's a wretched witch from Malaria Mountain."

"Alright, alright." All 'the brothers' laughed, even the gentleman in the bow-tie hollered.

"I think that sister likes you," said Supreme Justice looking in my direction. An enormous shiver went through my body.

Chapter 9

Revenge

"*F*orget about Brenda. Let's stay focused here. Understand? The place is Raul's Billiards Hall on Route 13. Ok? Everybody knows where that place is. We're not playing at Sam's Arcade as somebody suggested earlier because the place is too loud and I'm not putting my money on those raggedy tables. Understand? The time of the meeting is Saturday, high noon. Dragon hasn't lost a pool match in about two years. He even beat our Brother Intel from Roberto Clemente High School out of a hundred dollars last month from what my sources tell me. Hustling is what Dragon does best. He's walking into this match with a lot of confidence and he's been talking a lot of trash about the 5% Nation. We're not having that! With the help of the almighty Allah, young blood here can come through. That will definitely crush that out-of-control-ego of Dragon's and hopefully squash all this nonsense that our brother Knowledge Born has been going through at Northside in a peaceful nanner. Now, our brother Knowledge Born has agreed to vouch for this young blood, Grice. So, he takes on any and all debts that may be accrued during this match. Understand? As far as transportation, I need to know how all parties are getting to Raul's. We need to be early, so young blood here can practice a bit and get use to the tables they have over there. Let's make it 11 am. Understood?"

"How much money are we talking here, brother," asked the gentleman in the bow-tie as he lowered the volume on Farrakhan's speech.

"Right now it's two hundred, but I'm sure we can push it up to four. I want to break Dragon at his own game, in his own element, once and for all. Now that young blood here is taking Knowledge's place, we might even be able to bring it to five or more, who knows at this point. A lot of brothers said they want in on this thing. If we win you doubled your money," said Brother Star.

"Young blood? You're that good? Or are you just 'whistling Dixie'? If you don't do right in this match, these brothers aren't going to forget it," spoke the gentleman in the bow-tie. All 'the brothers' turned and looked at me.

"I played all the time for years in my ex-landlord's basement."

"For real? -- Put me in for 50 bucks Brother Star. I've haven't seen a good pool game in years. I'm definitely going to Raul's on Saturday. Where is it? Route 13 North? I'll be there. Here's my fifty," spoke the gentleman in the bow-tie as he stood up, reached in his wallet and pulled out a crisp fifty dollar bill. Brother Star took the bill, reached into his back pocket for his notepad and wrote it down.

"How do we know if Dragon is good for his losses," asked Supreme Justice.

"I called Raul this morning and he said he'd cover Dragon up to a thousand dollars. Raul's been stake horsing Dragon for the past two years and has made a lot of money off that fool. He's definitely hungry for this match to happen. Raul thinks his boy can't lose. -- Raul is a man of his word," answered Brother Star.

"I'll take Supreme and Universal up to Raul's on Saturday. I know their folks," said the gentleman in the bow-tie.

"I'm bringing some righteous cats with me on Saturday myself. I'm also going to contact Brother Intel about how Dragon plays, to give young blood here a heads up on how to play him. -- Knowledge Born, it's your responsibility to get young blood to Raul's. Understand?"

"Yes," replied Knowledge.

It was almost a quarter past four and I still didn't do my home-work. I quickly said my see-you-laters to Knowledge and 'the brothers' and walked past the statue. Newcleus' "Jam On It" blasted on the boom box and the break dancers were really putting an awe-some show. They had a nice crowd around them and the sun shined brightly.

Carver Park was only two blocks from the Evans' home and I definitely needed to play a few racks. I hadn't played in months. – As I walked to the Evans', I was hoping not to see Brenda again. I did wonder what she was doing at that particular moment, though. Was she doing her homework? What was watching TV with 'the God-sisters'? Maybe she was still at the park. Or maybe she's stirring a boiling hot cauldron of bat wings, spider legs and snake blood. One never knew with Brenda and Halloween was fast approaching.

RIINNNGGGG!!

"Ha-ha! What a sight for sore eyes. How ya been, kid," spoke Mr. Evans.

"I'm good. How are you, Mr. Evans?"

"I can't complain. Come on in. Make yourself at home, kid. How's your parents?"

"They're good."

"Boy, your father is one hard working man. -- You want some chopped barbeque? I just made some. Come over in the kitchen and learn something, kid. How's school?"

"School's good." I followed Mr. Evans into the kitchen. His chopped barbeque was always delicious.

"Always cook chopped barbeque nice and slow. If you don't you'll dry up all the flavor." I've heard Mr. Evans say that at least a hundred times before, as he reached inside the oven. It was definitely good to hear his voice again.

"Do you mind if I start my homework here while we talk?"

"Of course not. This is your home away from home. You're like a son to me, kid. You want some lemonade?"

"Ok. How's Roy and your oldest?"

"Rod is still stationed in Germany, you know. He's dating a white woman. I don't approve of that, you know, but it's his life. I didn't raise him like that, but I can't stop him. I guess he's doing good, thank the Lord. Roy... Roy is still looking for work. He signed up for a CDL school, you know, to teach him how to drive those big rigs. I'll pray for him. I can't do nothing but be thankful. God is good."

"All the time."

"I like that shirt you got on. Boy, your parents keep you neat. -- What type of homework you doing, kid?"

"Macbeth and some algebra."

Mr. Evans and I talked, ate barbeque and drank lemonade. He went in the living room to call my mom to let her know where I was then he sat and watched the news while I finished my homework. It was now approximately 5:30 pm.

"Let's shoot some pool, Mr. Evans."

"I thought you'd never ask. Let's go, kid. -- You rack 'em. I'll break 'em and make 'em."

We played pool until 8pm. My game was a tad off, but I felt rejuvenated. I asked Mr. Evans if I could borrow one of his fancy cue sticks and he said "Sure, kid." -- Mr. Evans drove me back to my parent's house and politely declined my mom's invitation to go inside for cake. Mr. Evans was a class act. I never told him about Brenda, 'the brothers' or my match with Dragon. Until this very day, I don't know why.

RIINNNGGGG!!

It was Friday, 6 am. I didn't want to go to school. I quickly scratched, stretched; and reached under my bed for my dad's birthday gift, which I bought and giftwrapped over the summer. It was a metal thermos and a bottle of cologne wrapped together in one box. That's all I could afford on my allowance. – I washed my face and walked downstairs. My mom was making pancakes and sausage. I could smell it before I got to the kitchen. My dad was still sleeping; he got home after midnight as always. I thought about what Knowledge said about sausage being evil and decided I would eat it anyway. Pancakes and sausage taste good, so if it's evil, hell mustn't be that bad, I thought quietly.

"Good morning, Grice. Don't forget to say 'Happy Birthday' to your father before you leave for school. Ok? "

"Good morning, Mom. I won't forget. I have dad's gift right here. Should I give him his present this morning or wait until later?"

"Why don't you go upstairs and see if your father is awake and surprise him. His boss finally let him have a day off today, so we'll be able to celebrate after I come home from work. Did you do all your homework?"

"Yeah."

"Oh, before I forget I bought you those two combination locks you asked for. I put them on the front door knob, so you or I wouldn't forget them."

"Thanks, mom."

"Go upstairs. Your pancakes won't freeze."

I slowly walked upstairs to my parent's room. I was nervous. My dad was almost a stranger to me. He worked so much I barely saw the man. I gently knocked on the door.

"Come in, son." His deep voice struck fear. I opened the door.

My dad was sitting on the edge of the bed in his sweat pants. He was holding an icepack to his right shoulder.

"Good morning, Dad. Happy birthday and many, many more." I handed him his gift.

"Thank you, son. How's everything?"

"Good."

"Your mom tells me you switched your major from welding to electronics. Is that what you wanted?"

"Yeah."

(pause) "Listen up, son...education is the key to a good life. It really is. I hope one day you can be your own boss... education... is truly the key."

"Ok."

"Ok. I'll see you later, son."

I rushed downstairs to eat my pancakes and evil sausages. My mom was in the living room ironing her suit jacket. It only took me seven minutes to eat three large pancakes, four little piggies and drink a glass of cold milk: my best personal best.

I quickly walked back upstairs and grabbed fresh undies and socks from my dresser and went into the shower. I started daydreaming again. I was a mighty billiards playing cyborg warrior sent here from the other side of the galaxy to save the universe from the ruthless intergalactic conqueror Dragonbeast. Laser blasters fired from my stainless steel cue stick as I stood on top of a crimson mountain. Lightning flashed in the orange sky... "Roar!!!! Grrrrrrrrrrr!!! I...am... the...greatest...pool...."

"Are you ok in there, Grice?"

"Yes, mom."

"Hurry up and get ready for school. Ok?"

"Ok."

After I showered and dressed, I walked into the living room just before my mom was set to leave for work.

"I just want you to know, Mom... that I appreciate you and I'm glad you're my mom."

"Oh, wow. Did you fall on your head or something? Do you need a doctor? Are you sure you're MY son? (haha) – Thank, you, Grice. Your father and I are very proud of you."

It was a rare treat that my father was in the car waiting to take me to school and my mom to work. Usually my mom, who didn't drive, took the bus to work and I walked to school. My dad's little navy blue Ford Mustang was his treasure and I was afraid to even fart in that car even if the windows were down.

RIINNNGGGG!!

It was the 8:10 am bell and the security guards instructed all Northside students to go inside the auditorium for a special announcement from Mrs. Brunswick, our principal. I had never seen so many kids jammed into a space so tightly. I quietly took my seat amongst the unruly energetic crowd. Knowledge wasn't there; he was late, as per usual. -- Vice Principal Tipp was a spiritually broken, miserable wretch of a man who detested all children and teachers alike. His whole vibe screamed it. He'd been in the educational field for too many years. Just walking into our school buildings made him flinch. Whenever the principal called for a meeting, he always sat in the same seat, playing his hiding-in-plain-sight role, in the front of the auditorium with a scowl on his face; never speaking in public settings as if he was allergic to his own position or some-thing. He was the most voiceless, powerless person of authority

I've ever meet. In sharp contrast, Mrs. Brunswick was a reasonably well liked, self-assured, glowing, personable woman who loved sashaying to the stage. A handful of diverse teachers happily stood with her.

"I'll wait until you're ready. (Pause). Hello students, staff, friends and parents. Will everyone please rise for the flag salute:

'I pledge allegiance, to the flag, of the United States of America, and to the republic for which it stands, one nation, under God, indivisible, with liberty and justice for all.'

Everyone please take your seats. I promise I won't take too long. I've gathered the school family here together this morning because I have exciting news and I also want to address any concerns about the shop majors that are available here at Northside. Once and for all you still have time to change your major if there is room to do so. -- There is especially good news for all the freshmen who have chosen business as their major...due to the overwhelming applications we've been receiving we will actually have two business shops. One will focus on banking and contemporary economics, the other on accounting and small business entrepreneurship. We've just hired a new business teacher as well for just that very reason. I also have another special announcement...drum roll please; we will be changing the name of our school from Northside High School to Northside Technical Institute. And in celebration of this momentous event I'm asking all the commercial artists of our school to design a brand new 'Mighty Lions' logo for our school's athletic teams. So, I'm excited about that and I'm 'like total-ly' looking forward to judging as well as selecting the new design. I think the new name and new logo will reflect a new beginning, one that hopefully requires all students to rise to the rigorous challenges and high expectations that face your generation. The school's colors: navy blue and gold will remain the same. Ok, Northside Technical Institute students, that's all I've got. Make sure you walk to your classes in a peaceful, orderly fashion; I don't want to send students to ISS this early in the school year. And don't forget, 'smile and the whole world will smile with you.'"

It was 8:30 am. I finally saw Knowledge about ten rows from me. He was with Brother Star and Supreme Justice. I walked in their direction.

"What's up, G-man? Everything good?"

"Everything's all set for Saturday, young blood, meaning that Dragon and his little snot nose crew are aware that you'll be standing in for Knowledge Born. Understand? I know some of you pool player-types like to psyche each other out before a match, so be on your toes today. Try to travel with other classmates in the hallway between classes; try not to do the loner thing, at least for today. Understand, young blood?"

"I understand," I said nervously. Did Dragon even know who I was? And what was HE thinking? Would Dragon and his minions really try to break my fingers before the match? I had a bunch of gloomy questions and a double dose of exhausting fear racing through my mind.

"Yo, G-man, the pot is up to eight hundred," whispered Knowledge as he punched his palm. He could barely contain his excitement.

"Just make sure that you bring your own pool stick, young blood. Dragon and his boys like to hide the good sticks at Raul's whenever they know a money game is coming their way. Understand?"

"I have one."

The security guards asked us to get to class pronto.

"Good. Young blood, make sure you bring it on Saturday. Understand? Go to class, we'll talk more later."

"Ok."

By then most of the students were outside the auditorium, moving into the hallway and scattering in different directions. I didn't see Dragon anywhere. I was now looking over both shoulders as I walked cautiously to Sociology. Supreme Justice, also a senior, was assigned to act as my first period bodyguard and escorted me three-fourths of the way to class. "Eight hundred dollars? 'Stay on my toes'? Wow. What in the world am I in for next," I asked myself quietly.

Chapter 10

Good Vs. Evil

"**G**ood morning, class," spoke Mrs. Ball.

"Good morning, Mrs. Ball," spoke the class, some in a mocking tone.

"Well, we finished watching 'The Verdict,' yesterday, didn't we? Oh dear, I haven't taken attendance yet, have I? Let...me...yes, here it is. Is everyone here? Let's see now...I have twenty on my list and 2, 4, 6... yyyes, everyone's here. Great. Now, where was I? Yes, 'The Verdict'...what did you students think?"

"It was a very interesting look at how lawyers...are, well, real people with real problems and responsibilities, both personally and professionally," spoke one student.

"I thought it was a really good movie because it showed how

serious it is to be in a courtroom, whether you're a lawyer, a judge, a witness or a jury member," I said.

"It's better than most movies I've seen," said another student.

"I didn't like the part where Frank Gavin slaps the woman to the floor. If that was me, I would've slapped him back or something," said one girl.

"She totally used him and, like...sold him out to his enemies, though," said another girl. "She deserved worse than that in my opinion."

"Well, attorneys on opposing sides of a particular case aren't always personal enemies," Mrs. Ball interjected. "As a matter of fact, attorneys on opposite sides of a difficult medical malpractice case, such as the one in the film, often can learn from each other's legal styles. - Did you think that Frank Gavin's slapping of the woman who was paid to spy on his strategy and plaintiff's information, then handing over that information to the defense was the greatest evil in the film?"

"No," the class said collectively.

"How would you define 'good' or 'evil'?" asked Mrs. Ball.

"Good is helping someone in need," said one boy.

"Ok," replied Mr. Ball. "So, do you think Frank Gavin is good or evil?"

"I think he's a good character because he's trying to fight for the woman who was paralyzed by an evil doctor," explained one girl.

"I see. How can Frank Gavin be a 'good' man if he's also the type of man who drinks too much and does in fact strike a poor, defenseless woman to the floor in a crowded hotel bar?" asked a very tricky Mrs. Ball.

"I guess everyone has a good side and an evil side to their own personality," I said. "I just think Frank Gavin is more good than evil, like most people."

"What about the woman, Laura is her name in the film, who gets slapped? Is she evil?"

"Yes," said most of the class, including myself. Some said "No."

"Why?"

"She's definitely evil because she leads Frank Gavin to believe that...she really likes him and all that, but she's really only using him," said one student.

"So, from YOUR point-of-view, you see Laura as 'evil.' What if Laura is only selling Frank Gavin out because she needs the money for some good cause like to help her sick mother or donate to cancer research? Is she still evil?"

"Yes," shouted one student.

"Why?"

"Doing something wrong to do something right is still wrong," said another. "That's like me stealing an old lady's purse to feed my little sister."

"Shhhoe! If my little sister is starving to death I WOULD steal an old lady's purse! What else can you do?" shouted one student.

"You can get a job, or ask people for help, stupid!!!" shouted one girl. The whole class erupted with laughter; students began losing focus and talking over each other.

"Okay class, that's enough," said Mrs. Ball calmly. "I just wanted this class to really think about the world in which we live. We really don't live in a world of absolute good and absolute evil, do we? We live in the middle somewhere; a gray area if you will. I think "The Verdict" is a wonderful film about the complexity of good vs.

evil; the powerful vs. the power less and all the shadows and chess moves that lie underneath. Paul Newman is one of my favorite actors and in this film he's never been better, in my opinion. – So, for the rest of the period, you're going to write a small paragraph on what you liked or didn't like about this film. And I want you to think beyond the traditional preconceived notions of good and evil, ok? You can go to my desk if you need loose leaf paper." Everyone got up and retrieved a single sheet. Mrs. Ball didn't mind students walking around or choosing their own groups to sit in. She encouraged students to share their ideas with one another and as a result Mrs. Ball's classroom was, for the most part, very relaxed and stress free. I loved having her class for first period.

 RIINNNGGGG!!

 I quickly finished my paragraph on how I thought Frank Gavin was a 'good' lawyer that desperately needed redemption; the character of Frank Gavin isn't perfect, but perfection isn't required for moral transformation. I could hear Pastor McDonaldson's professor–like voice guiding my hand as I wrote. I closed my paragraph with a line I remembered from one of Pastor McDonaldson's sermons, "Being a good Christian is more than the study of eschatology; it's the study of repentance." There. Done. I grabbed my book bag and hurried to my second period class, Mr. Connelly's Western Civilization. As I walked the hallways of Northside, thoughts of good and evil swirled in my mind. Was there 'good' in a guy like Dragon? Maybe Dragon was a poor misunderstood kid from the ghetto like me. I began to think that Dragon wasn't nearly as bad as I made him out to be in my mind. A huge calm blanketed me as I walked into Mr. Connelly's classroom. I hadn't seen Dragon all morning; I became less paranoid. Maybe Dragon wasn't in school today. Maybe Dragon was afraid to face me in a pool challenge, I thought quietly.

RIINNNGGGG!!

I was just sitting down as the late bell sounded for second period. Mr. Connelly was sitting behind his desk; cool and observant as usual. Students were talking in their whispering voices as they sat and organized themselves.

"Hi Grice," spoke Jennifer Gooden as she waved from the front corner seat. She was dressed in a fancy green blouse and matching skirt.

"Hi Jennifer. How's it going?" I asked as I tried to get comfortable in my chair.

"Good," she replied warmly. Mr. Connelly quickly glanced at Jennifer Gooden and then back at me and slightly smiled.

"Almost everyone did well on yesterday's quiz, (pause)

I once married a heartless woman named Liz, We later divorced and now she works in show biz..." Everyone laughed. Mr. Connelly continued. "I want to talk a little bit about the Constitution and focus particularly on The Bill of Rights today if I can. I like this class and I feel we can cover a lot of ground and engage in some pretty interesting dialogue."

Mr. Connelly calmly stood up, slowly walked to the front of his desk and leaned on the top with his arms and legs folded. "The Constitution of the United States is the supreme law of this nation.' Mr. Connelly explained as students were writing to keep up. 'The first three Articles of the Constitution establish our country's three brands of government. Can anyone name one?"

"The legislature," replied Jennifer Gooden.

"That's correct. The legislature branch is represented by

Congress," spoke Mr. Connelly. "The next branch is represented by the president of the United States and that branch is called…"

"The executive," said Hector Velasquez.

"Correct. And the third branch is the judicial branch which is represented by…"

"The Supreme Court," I said.

"Yes, Mr. pool player extraordinaire,' spoke Mr. Connelly. A few students chuckled. 'That's also correct. Good job. Now for Article Four of the Constitution: Article Four outlines the relationship between the states and our federal government." Students were writing at a frantic pace. Mr. Connelly continued…

"Now, before I go any further and start unpacking The Bill of Rights, which I promise I'll get to … I want someone to success-fully articulate, if they can, what they believe the purpose of our Constitution serves…"

"To unite and protect the interest of rich white property owners," I said. My classmates were silent.

"In the beginning, that was true. – The Constitution was first proposed on September 17, 1787 by what was known as the

Constitutional Convention which had chief delegates like James Madison and Alexander Hamilton. George Washington was elected by the delegates to preside over the convention. This historic convention took place in Philadelphia, Pennsylvania. There were later ratifications by other individual state conventions. If I'm going too fast let me know (pause). There have been over two dozen amendments to the Constitution; the first ten are known as the Bill of Rights. The Bill of Rights and other amendments were added to create a more perfect union and protect all Americans, not just rich white property owners." I could hear all the heavy writing on the desks; it sounded like a group of grizzly bears scratching their backs on trees.

"Was George Washington president of the United States when the Constitution was conceived?" asked one student.

"Good question. No, George Washington was not president of our country at that time. The creation of the Constitution basically gave birth to the United States of America. A true president could not have existed without it. George Washington became president two years after, in 1789 and he remained president until 1797." As

Mr. Connelly paused to let students catch up, a student from the Commerical Art room walked in with an original portrait of Dr. King. Some of the students ooo'd and aah'd.

"Thank you. Tell Mr. Murphy, I said 'It's about time,'" said Mr. Connelly.

"Ok," said the art student as he left.

"That's totally awesome," said one girl about the portrait.

"That's cool," said one boy.

"Last year, at the White House Rose Garden our current president, Ronald Reagan signed a bill to make a federal holiday honoring the legacy of Dr. King," spoke Mr. Connelly. "That would make him the first black American and the first private citizen to have a federal holiday. My good pal, Murph, the art teacher promised to have one of his seniors from last year lend me this portrait for my upcoming history display. So, here we are..."

"Did you ever march with Dr. King, Mr. Connelly?" asked one student.

"Even when I was younger, I understood the importance of the Civil Rights Movement, equal Rights and Dr. King's work; his eloquence, intelligence and 'dream' really captured so many people's imaginations and hearts, both black and white; it really was a pivotal moment in American history and a tremendous triumph of a nonviolent revolution, but no. Sadly, I never actually marched with him or to Washington on that famous day when he delivered that 'I Have a Dream' speech. There'll never be another leader like that in my life time, I don't think."

"What about Minister Louis Farrakhan? I think he's a strong leader who people should pay attention to, too," I said. I saw a few eyes roll and heard a few sighs, but the most of the class was alert and still.

"Well first off... I don't follow Farrakhan that closely, but I believe Farrakhan preaches racial separatism which, in my humble opinion, is the wrong approach to fighting racism and classism. Secondly, I think his association with Jesse Jackson ruined Jackson's potential of being a serious presidential candidate or even being considered for a possible Vice Presidential choice in the Democratic Party, which is a real shame. I also believe it is a great benefit to blacks, and yes whites too, to have the very best and brightest of all colors and backgrounds working together intelligently and cohesively to form a stronger America. That's what I believe Dr. King's work and legacy reflects; a belief that 'all men are created equal.' Third, I think separatism would only create more distrust, more anger, and more problems between the races. What do you think?"

"I think that black people can't survive in a racist, classist, lopsided society and eventually black people will be crushed under the weight of that lopsidedness in a long, dragged out sad fashion. The odds of a people who have suffered and sacrificed so unjustly, thriving in this system are overwhelming."

"I believe, with the help of... good parents, a quality education, and a POSITIVE OUTLOOK, Mr. Poolplayer, a people, no matter their color can persevere and achieve anything. When my parents came to this country from Ireland, things weren't easy for them. They had to work, save, and fight to keep their dreams of a better future for their family alive. A true leader provides his people with a sense of inspiration and hope, not doom and gloom. Hope is the most powerful weapon on Earth. "

RIINNNGGGG!!

I slowly put my Western Civilization notebook and pen in my book bag as the classroom emptied out. Jennifer Gooden waited for me at the door. Mr. Connelly's words still swirling through my frontal and parietal lobes.

"I thought you were incredible back there, Grice," said a visibly excited Jennifer Gooden.

"Thanks. I was alright, I guess. Mr. Connelly was smooth, though. Did you see that?"

"I thought you were, too. - I got Science. What do you have now?"

"I have English Composition with Mrs. Sla..."

"Hi, Bagel Boy! What's new in the world of the emotionally repressed?!!" yelled Brenda from across the hall.

I turned my back to Brenda as she walked down the hallway toward me and ignored her.

"Yeah, Jennifer...I have Mrs. Slate for English now. I hope I can see you later."

"Yeah, in gym class. Ok, Grice. See you later," spoke Jennifer Gooden as she waved gently and walked away. Her cotton candy-filled spirit lingered and filled my lungs. As I turned back around to watch her walk away, Brenda rolled her eyes at Jennifer Gooden with a scrunched face as she walked pass her walking straight to me. I braced myself for the impact.

"Ooooo, Bagel Boy. Who is that?! That's your girlfriend?"

"Why do you always…"

"She looks like a country bumpkin if you ask me. That's perfect for you! Haha! I'm telling your mother, you have a girlfriend, Bagel Boy!"

All of a sudden, a tall skinny kid with a gold tooth and stutter approached me, stopping my rebuttal to 'Big Mouth' Brenda…

"Are you, you, you G, G-man?"

"Yes," I replied.

The gold toothed kid shoved me hard to the floor and kicked me in my stomach twice. Everyone the hallway, including Brenda watched in shock.

"D-Death is c-coming your way. Tha, that's a mess, message from Da, Da, Dragon!!" The gold toothed kid quickly ran down the stairway and disappeared. Security was nowhere to be found.

"Are you ok, Bagel Boy? What was that all about? Do you know that kid?" asked Brenda as she helped me up from the floor.

"(ugh) No, I don't know that kid."

"Who's Da, Da, Dragon?" asked Brenda trying to lighten my mood.

"A kid I'm supposed to play against in a pool match on Saturday at Raul's at 12," I replied without concern for manly honor or secrecy.

"Are you sure you're ok? Do you need to go to the nurse or something? You should report that."

"I'm ok."

"Well, um, ok then. I didn't know you played pool. Um, we'd better get to Mrs. Slate's class before we're late."

"Ok."

As Brenda and I walked through the crowd, still whispering about me being shoved and kicked, we entered Mrs. Slate's classroom without another word uttered between us. Mrs. Slate yelled over Chapter 2 in Macbeth and I would sit throughout English Composition in a daze; I couldn't even daydream. My stomach still hurt. When I travelled to Mr. Bassford's class my stomach hurt even worst.

There was an argument boiling over in the Science room. I could hear the shouting even before I entered the classroom. It was between Mr. Bassford and a junior named Benita Patel. She was infuriated. The whole class was amused.

"How could you give me a zero and take away my marble?!!!" shouted Benita.

"You placed a yellow handout sheet in a green folder. That's absolutely forbidden and you know that, Benita."

"You are a total jerk! What difference does it make?!!! It's just a folder!!!"

"I spend a lot of time making sure all the classes' folders are properly numbered, labeled and differentiated by color. You are deliberately being dissident!! Now, run along and let me teach my class!!"

"You still didn't answer my question?! Why all this fuss over a stupid folder?!! Maybe you don't even know!!!"

"What part of 'get out' don't you understand?!! Not only won't you get your marble back, I'm going to make sure I minus ten points off your final grade of the marking period!!!"

"I'm going to report you to Mrs. Brunswick and Mr. Tipp!!!" yelled Benita as she stormed away.

"Good!! I've got tenure; they can't do anything to me!!!" Mr. Bassford's eye was twitching franticly and veins were forming on the sides of his head. The class immediately got super silent. After several uncomfortable minutes, Mr. Bassford passed out the new science textbooks and told the students to read Chapter five and do the questions at the end. My stomach felt a little a bit better.

RIINNNGGGG!!

I really wasn't in an athletic mindset as I walked to gym class. I was cautiously alert as I strolled the hallways of Northside and started to think. How did Dragon and his posse know who I was so quickly? Did someone rat me out? Was I being set up? God knew the answer but I didn't really know for sure.

As I got dressed in the locker room, I could see Knowledge approaching me. I was guarded.

"What's up, G-man?"

"Someone pushed me to the floor and kicked me in the hallway after second period."

"Today? Who? What did he look like?"

"Yeah, today. Some skinny kid with a gold tooth."

"That's Multiple. He got that name 'cause…"

"Yeah. I know. It doesn't matter."

"Don't worry, G-man. I got your back."

"Yeah? Do you really?"

"What's that supposed to mean, G-man? You're my boy."

"I just can't wait until Saturday is over with."

"I hear ya, G-man! Brother Star said the pot is now a thousand dollars. A thousand, G-man! You'd better win! - I hear the gym teachers lining the students up. Let's get going."

"Yeah."

RIINNNGGGG!!

"Ok. Line up on the black line! Quiet down! It's Friday and all the students who are prepared can pick their sport. You can play basketball on the court, play catch with the gloves over here, or run on the indoor track. Just don't touch the ropes or pull-up bars without being properly supervised," said Ms. Gomez. "On three, 1, 2, 3..."

"I WILL TRY!!!!!"

I ran to the baseball gloves and played catch with a long, haired head-banger with a Van Halen shirt. He was cool. Knowledge played basketball. I glanced to see if I could spot Jennifer Gooden. She was chatting and giggling with a couple of girls in the corner of the gym. She glanced back in my direction. Our eyes met; my heart did a back flip.

RIINNNGGGG!!

Gym class went quick. I was definitely hungry; but my mind was worrisome. Was Dragon or Multiple waiting for me in the cafeteria? Could I trust Knowledge or 'the brothers'? I was truly afraid and I needed to talk with somebody. I didn't want any more surprises.

Chapter 11

The Match

I roamed the second floor far away from the café and noticed the teacher's lounge. I knew I'd be safe from the madness in there. I slowly opened the door.

"Trust me... Walter Mondale with Geraldine Ferraro as Vice President isn't going to win the election. This country isn't ready for a woman that's that close to 'the nuclear button,'" said one teacher.

"I personally LIKED John Glenn, but...WELL do YOU want Ronald Reagan...HEY... KID, this room is OFF LIMITS," yelled Mrs. Slate noticing me peeking through the doorway. She was talking with a mouth full of pizza; crumbs were all over her shirt.

"Is Mr. Connelly here?" I asked.

"Hey, Jimmyl! You got a kid here to see you! Just wait outside, he'll meet you out there," said Mrs. Slate noticing I was one of her students.

"Ok."

I waited in the hallway, looking at one of a American Literature teacher's bulletin boards for only a minute when I could hear the teacher's lounge door creek open. I turned around and spoke first.

"Hi, Mr. Connelly. Can I talk to you for a minute or two, privately?"

"Sure, Grice. Let's go to my classroom."

"Ok."

We started walking to his classroom which was only around the corner. Mr. Connelly carried his brown paper lunch bag with him.

"I enjoyed our earlier exchange this morning. It's rare for me that any student of mine rises critical philosophical questions or ideas in the classroom. Keep those ideas coming. You're off to a good start. Keep up the good work."

"Thanks." I was stunned. We arrived at Mr. Connelly's classroom. He unlocked the door. We walked inside. Mr. Connelly sat at his desk and unpacked a turkey sandwich and a Dr. Pepper. He took out a small mustard packet from his top draw. I sat in the front desk facing him.

"So, young man...what's on your mind?"

"Do you know who Dragon is? He's a student here."

"Sure. That's Chauncey Fogle. I had the terrible misfortune of having him for a student last year. Every teacher in this building knows who he is. He's a troubled little piss ant with an anger problem. He's been suspended for fighting already and this is just the first week. What's the story, kid?"

"Somehow I managed to talk myself into a jam. Tomorrow I have a pool match at Raul's against Dragon. There's money involved and I can't back down. It's at high noon. I'm scared."

"I see...now, when I first met you, you said ...and I'm quoting here, 'I can beat anyone. I'm the best.' Now, were you just blowing smoke or are you...?"

"I've played pool since I was a small child! Cisero Murphy is one of my heroes. I played all the time in my old house with my land-lord. I can really play, Mr. Connelly!"

"Now, that's what I wanted to hear you say! No need to be scared then. Walk into that match with confidence. Go to Raul's and play your best game, that's all. It'll be ok. Alright?"

"Ok. Thanks, Mr. Connelly. I feel a lot better."

"Not a problem. - Aren't you supposed to be eating lunch at this time?"

"Yeah, but I'm not really hungry."

"You know, my wife makes the worst turkey sandwiches. I keep telling her to buy the good meat at Ed's Deli. But, she insists on buying that cheap stuff at the supermarket. I've got to drown out the taste with mustard. Kid, don't ever get married," said Mr. Connelly as he opened another packet. I laughed.

RIINNNGGGG!!

Mr. Connelly asked me to join the new debating team he was starting at Northside and I said I would think about it. I headed toward Algebra 1 with Mr. Q. I still didn't have my locker number, so I couldn't ditch my book bag. As I guarded myself, I walked to class and thought about The Lord's Prayer...

The Lord is my Shepherd, I shall not want.

He makes me lie down in green pastures,

He leads me beside quiet waters, He restores my soul.

He guides me in paths of righteousness for His name's sake.

Even though I walk through the valley of the shadow of death,

I will fear no evil, for You are with me;

Your rod and Your staff, they comfort me.

You prepare a table before me in the presence of my enemies.

You anoint my head with oil; my cup overflows.

Surely goodness and love will follow me all the days of my life,

And I will dwell in the house of the Lord forever.

Amen.

I didn't know all the angles yet, however my gut was fine now. I was early and sat in my seat along with half the class. I took out my Algebra book and pretended to be studying. I started to daydream again. – I was a sheriff, beaten and tied up inside a jail by the evil cattle rancher Dragon and his twisted stuttering gunman sidekick Multiple. They were planning to rob a train and tied the beautiful Jennifer Gooden to the train tracks as a means to slow it down. My deputy Knowledge was nowhere to be found. I hid a small knife in my cowboy boot. If only I could reach it...

RIINNNGGGG

"Good afternoon, everyone," spoke Mr. Q.

"Good afternoon," replied the whole class respectfully.

"I went into the boy's restroom earlier today and I noticed someone wrote something on the wall...it said 'The Polish are Moorans' and I thought hmmm...that's interesting. Now, either the idiot who scribbled that garbage on the wall thinks polish people, who are quite intelligent and good looking by the way, believe in the ritual purity of shaving a baby's hair according to Hindu customs or the fool meant to write the word 'moron' and couldn't spell it properly. Either way, I thought THAT was funny and I felt like sharing it with my beloved students.' The students laughed nervously. 'Did everyone do their homework? Of course you did," continued Mr. Q without skipping a beat. Mr. Q. reviewed our homework and went over linear equations and functions. We also started making graphs. I breezed through that period like a master mechanic doing an oil change. - I couldn't believe how fast the day was going. I actually wanted 'Father Time' to tap the brakes.

As I walked through the Joseph P. Torello, Jr. Building to Mr. R.

Torello's Electronics class I couldn't stop thinking about Saturday. I daydreamed some more. I was walking into a graveyard of fallen pool players. People were standing over one grave in particular. I walked closer. People were ignoring me; they were weeping. I looked inside the grave and it was...

RIINNNGGGG!!

I walked into Electronics and sat in the front as I always did. I was early again and the seniors were still gathering their odometers and other tools to clear out the shop for the freshmen. Mr. Torello was outside talking with a female teacher and finishing a cigarette. I noticed something on Mr. Torello's desk that I hadn't previously. It was a small faded illustrated picture of Saint Francis of Assisi; there were words typed underneath. It read: "It is in pardoning others, we are pardoned." I only glanced at the picture for a few seconds and admittedly I didn't fully comprehend the caption in its totality at first, however those eight not-so-simple words have shaped and continue to shape my philosophy on life.

Mr. Torello stomped out his cigarette, parted ways with the other teacher and re-entered the shop. Most of the freshmen students were on time and ready to dive into more talk about the founding fathers of electronics. Mr. Torello had other ideas. He told the students to go into the work table area where there were disassembled computers and calibration machines. We were given new texts books and studied color codes, capacitors and motherboards. I struggled to keep up. Knowledge and I avoided each other the whole shop period.

RIINNNGGGG!!

Just before we left shop, Mr. Torello informed the freshmen that we would be getting our locker location numbers on Monday, to bring a strong combination lock and to never put anything in our lockers that we didn't want our grandmothers to see.

I waited outside the shop for any instructions that would be forthcoming from Knowledge or 'the brothers'. Knowledge simply said he would see me on Saturday at Raul's and left in Brother Star's car. There were no instructions. No 'good luck on Saturday'. No 'I hope you do well young man'. There was nothing. No inspiring words at all. I never felt so alone or alienated.

The walk home seemed to last forever. I wanted to practice again and talk to Mr. Evans, but I knew I needed a restful night's sleep for tomorrow match. When I arrived home my dad's Mustang wasn't there; I made myself a bologna and cheese sandwich and watched Voltron followed by the ThunderCats in the living room which were filled with balloons for my dad's birthday; the cake was in the frig.' I tried desperately to take my mind off of the upcoming match with Dragon. I wondered what Dragon was doing at that moment. Was he practicing at Raul's? Was he as worried as I was? If I loss what was going to happen to ME? I went into my room upstairs and played with my Star Wars action figures and re-read some of my Captain America comic books. I replayed Mr. Connelly's encouraging words over in my head. I wanted my mind to relax. I thought about all the things Mr. Evans thought me about relaxing and playing loose and focused. I thought about Brenda and Jennifer Gooden and how different they were from each other. I walked back downstairs into the living room again and opened the large family bible located on my dad's piano. According to my mom, when my dad was younger, he wanted to be a jazz piano player, not unlike Thelonious Monk or Billy Preston. Sometimes on Sundays when my dad wasn't working a double shift he would play.

When I opened the bible, I was surprised to find so many folded down corners and highlighted text. One story in particular captured my eye: The Book of Jonah. It tells how God directs Jonah to inform the Ninevites to repent or suffer due to their wickedness. However, Jonah has his own ideas and decides to take off for Tarshish with a team of sailors instead. God isn't pleased. A storm attacks Jonah's ship and he knows why. Jonah tells the sailors to toss him overboard in order to save their own lives. They do exactly that. As Jonah is drowning at sea, a great fish swallows him. Jonah suffers in darkness and uncertainty for three days, but is alive. In those days Jonah prays and is genuinely grateful to be alive, even though he's in the belly of a beast. After three days, the great fish regurgitates Jonah back on land in good health and in renewed spirit. –Pastor McDonaldson mentioned Jonah a few times in his sermons, but this was my first time reading and interpreting the story for myself. I was now getting tried. My mind was finally exhausted and I needed sleep. It was 7pm and my mom usually got home at 6. Maybe my parents went somewhere to celebrate my dad's birthday together.

I walked back upstairs to put a warm washcloth on the back of my neck. That always helped me go to sleep. I got in my bed. It was dark outside and still. My eyes were heavy, but I could hear my dad's Mustang move across the driveway blacktop. I perked up some as I knew they probably brought home some Chinese food from around the corner. My mom didn't like cooking late into the night. Besides, I was hungry for some strawberry shortcake; that was dad's favorite cake. Mine, too.

"GRICE!!" called my mom.

"Yeah."

"Get down here. We got some Chinese."

"Ok."

I ran downstairs, washed my hands at the kitchen sink and passed out the plates and forks. My mom put the cake in the center of the dining room table. My dad read a passage from the large family bible...

"The grass withers and the flowers fall, but the word of our God stands forever." (Isaiah 40:8).

We ate General's Tso chicken and vegetable fried rice while

listening to Smokey Robinson and Lou Rawls records.

"How's school, Grice?" asked my mom.

"Good."

"How do you like that electronics shop, son? Is everything ok?"

"Everything's good."

"Mr. Connelly called me this afternoon," said my dad as he scooped a forkful. He was totally calm.

"Huh?" I said as my big piece of red chicken dropped off my fork.

"Yeah. One of your teachers called me about some pool match you're having tomorrow at some place on Route 13 North."

"Oh, that thing. Yeah, I, I forgot to tell you guys, haha, that I have a pool match at this place called 'Raul's Pool Hall' on Route 13."

"We don't like secrets, Grice. You should and can come to us about anything. We shouldn't have…"

"I know mom…"

"How were you going to get to Raul's, son?"

"By bus. The 158 goes right pass there."

"Son, you should never walk into a place that you've never been, playing a match with people you don't really know...anything can happen to you. You're OUR son! Do you understand that?"

"Yes."

"We're not upset with you, Grice. You just need to understand how serious a situation this can turn into..."

"Ok."

"I know I've been working a lot of hours lately, but son you must tell us what's going with you. - I told Mr. Burton that I'm also taking the day off tomorrow. So, I'll be taking you to this Raul's place, ok? You're not walking into that situation without your father. Period."

"Was Mr. Burton ok when you asked him for the extra day off?" asked my mom.

"I didn't ask, honey...I told him I needed to be with my family. That's it. He has a family, he should understand where I'm coming from. I'll work my doubles on Sunday and Monday, we do need the money, but this is important. People need to know that my son has back-up."

"You're absolutely right, honey. - Do you have anything to add,

Grice?" asked my mom.

"No."

My mom asked me to cut the cake. No one bothered with candles; and we ate slices of delicious strawberry shortcake while listening to Marvin Gaye's "What's Going On." I felt relieved about going to Raul's with my father. At least, I didn't have to worry about getting shoved and kicked in Raul's or God knows what else. - It was now very late and my Whitney Houston poster and fresh sheets were calling my name. I fell fast asleep.

RIINNNGGGG

I wanted to break my alarm clock with a hammer. It was 6:30am and my parents were already up talking in the living room. They were talking with regular voices, but I could hear them through the walls. Children always hear their parents through the walls.

"Son, you up?" asked my dad from downstairs. He probably heard my alarm clock holler.

"Yeah."

"Just throw on some sweatpants and your sneakers, ok?"

"Ok." I threw on my dark gray sweatpants and blue T-shirt from my dresser and put on my old white Ponies. I washed my face and brushed my teeth in the master bathroom and walked cautiously downstairs.

"Good morning, son. How do you feel?"

"Good morning, dad."

"I want us to go for a little jog this morning before it gets too hot outside, ok? I need to replenish my energy level. -- We'll do a little jog through Douglass Park then eat our breakfast. What do you think?"

"Ok," I said. Douglass Park was only five blocks from our new home.

My father and I lightly jogged through Douglass Park in what seemed to be a grueling marathon of winding roads and hills. My shins and lungs were on fire. In reality we probably jogged closer to two and a half miles that morning. When we walked back home, my mom had homemade cornbread and bacon on the stove. It was still warm.

It was now a quarter past eight. My father and I finished eating our breakfast and drank our apple juice while my mom sang as she did laundry in her new sanctuary, the cellar. -- I hit the showers.

After I cleaned up, I stood in my room starring inside my closet. What should I wear to this pool match? I started daydreaming again. I was a scared kid falsely accused and arrested by the evil King Dragon and thrown into a lion's den. I had no armor. No shield. No sword. As the lions gathered and walked toward me, I...

Knock, knock!!

"Son? Come downstairs when you're ready, ok?"

"Ok."

I quickly put on my favorite jeans and casual shoes. I wasn't sure about the shirt, but I eventually settled on comfort over style and threw on my plain pale blue short-sleeve golf shirt. – I ran downstairs.

"Son, I want us to watch a little western film classic I picked up from the video store. It's called 'The Magnificent Seven.' It has a bunch of stars in it, like Yul Brenner, Steve McQueen, and James Coburn, people like that. I think you'll like it...let's just watch a little of it and see, ok?"

"Ok," I answered.

We watched the movie until about ten thirty. My dad went upstairs to get his car keys and jacket. My mom walked downstairs with him. I had Mr. Evan's pool case already at my side.

"Good luck, Grice. I know you'll do well," my mom said.

"Thanks." My palms began to sweat.

The day was humid but clouds were beginning to form. My father and I stepped into the Mustang. The engine roared. Thunder screamed at the sky. A few raindrops bombed the windshield. I could feel my heart racing faster.

"Where did you get the pool case, son? Mr. Evans?"

"Yeah."

"Don't worry, son. Just do your best, ok? Everything will be fine."

"Ok."

"Is your friend Kevin going to be there?"

"Yeah. He changed his name to Knowledge Born."

"I see. Just remember son, a man doesn't need a fancy name to become someone in life. Believing in Jesus, hard work and maintaining a good reputation can take a man pretty far,

ok?"

"Ok."

"Did you like the film?"

"Yeah. I think the characters are cool. I liked the character Britt, the quiet guy that carries a switchblade. I also like the musical score."

"Yeah, the musical score is pretty famous. It was done by Elmer Bernstein."

Chapter 12

Dragon Destroys Bagel Boy

As we talked with Motown records playing softly on the car radio, the sky darkened and the rain become heavy. My father made a left from Graham Street onto Route 13 North and turned on the air to clear the thick fog sticking to the windshield. Lightning shredded the sky. It was a few minutes pass eleven. The giant Exxon station was just ahead. My father pulled into the parking lot of a wide two-floor building with a neon sign that read 'Raul's'. There were several cars in the lot and two bicycles chained under the canopy. One the bicycles had a cartoon picture of a faded wicked-looking dragon with six horns between its handle bars. This was my first trip to a real pool hall. The insides of my chest tightened. My father parked near the front entrance, pulled up the emergency brake and shut the engine off. The rain came down in barrels. Except for the heavy rain, there was total silence in the car.

"We're going to practice a bit, son. You know, before..."

"Ok."

With that said, both of us bolted from the Mustang and ran into Raul's. – It was almost like a ghost town at first. No one seemed to be inside. There were twelve shiny table shattered throughout the first floor. There was well groomed brown carpeting, pictures of famous pool players on the wall, and a large Dominican Republic flag hanged over a roped off lonely well- kept table just to the right by the rest rooms. There was no one at the check-in desk. My father rang the front desk bell. A short dark-skinned man with a heavy Spanish accent and bright smile walked from behind a curtain and answered politely.

"Hello. Good morning. My name is Raul Perez. This is my place along with my brother Javier. Please call me, Raul. How can I help you?"

"Good morning, Mr. Raul. My son here, has a scheduled match here at 12 noon today. Is there a table we can practice on until that time, sir?"

"Oh, of course. No problem. I've wasn't sure if the match was going to be cancelled because of all the rain. Yes, of course. Please choose the table you want. Your son's opponent is upstairs practicing too."

"How much are your tables, sir?"

"Nooo. There's no charge for the practice time before a match in my place. Choose your table. No problem."

"Thank you, sir."

My father and I walked to table # 1 and we grabbed two of the sticks which were located on the wall. Brother Star was right, the sticks were beat up and most were warped so badly they could've been used as archery bows. I was glad I had borrowed Mr. Evans' cue stick. It was a beauty, too.

"These sticks are horrible huh, son. It a good thing you brought one here. Wow. Ok, let me see that stick, son." I handed my father the pool cue. He admired the weight and checked the balance with a nod of approval.

"We'll just use this one I guess then, son."

"Ok. I want to use one of the beat up sticks to break with."

"I don't know, son. I don't believe there's a straight stick in the house. I think you're better off using the same stick to break with, ok."

"Yeah. You're right."

I wanted to practice my straight in shots, so my father lined up the stripes and solids diagonally across the table. The speed on the table was fast and I had to adjust my technique accordingly.

My stomach was as restless as a one-eyed squirrel surrounded by anacondas. – As I practiced with my father I could see two sets of headlights approaching the parking lot through the rain drenched windows. One car was the Ford Thunderbird from Carver Park. The gentleman with the bow-tie, Universal, Supreme Justice and a beautiful woman stepped out of that one. The other was the Chevy Nova. Brother Star, Knowledge and...Brenda along with Georgette walked out of that one. I thought I was going to faint.

"Yo, G-Man! What's up? You brought your pops, G-man??? Cool."

"Hey, young blood."

"Hi, Bagel Boy! Hi, Mr. Grafton!"

"Hi. This is my dad. We're just practicing until the match starts."

"Alright, alright."

"Nice to meet you, Mr. Grafton," said Brother Star.

"Nice to meet all of you," replied my father.

"Hey, where's Raul hiding?!! Hey, Raul...you back there?!!" asked Brother Star.

"Hello. Good morning. I'm Raul. You must be Brother Star. Dragon and one of his friends are upstairs. They'll be down when the match starts. Everyone can sit on either the sofas or stools. We'll play on the roped off table by the restrooms, here, when we begin... this should be in about five minutes."

I could see another pair of headlights approaching the building. It was silver Honda Accord. Mr. Connelly and a teenage boy with braces and a T-shirt that read 'Fighting Irish' stepped out and ran inside.

"Hey, Mr. Connelly," I said.

"Hey, Mr. Pool player...and this must be your father. How are you, sir?"

"I'm fine. - You didn't want to miss this match either, huh?" my father said in jest.

"Not for the world."

< My father and Mr. Connelly shook hands. >

"This is my son, Sean. He's been begging me to buy a pool table for our den area, ((whispering voice)) but my wife won't allow it," continued Mr. Connelly. My father and Mr. Connelly both laughed. – There was also loud laughter coming from upstairs. The place got quiet for a moment. I could hear footsteps thundering down the stairs. It was Dragon and Multiple. Both were dressed in black jeans, Pumas with the fat laces and large gold chains over crisp black T-shirts. Fear gripped my soul.

"(Humph). Where's Jellyfish? Yo, Jellyfish, after I destroy your man in this match I'm gonna buy you a donut just to show these slobs how charitable I can be."

"Ye, ye, yeah (hahaha)!"

"No time for talk now, Dragon. Time to put up," spoke Knowledge.

"(Humph). 'Time to make the donuts' eh, Jellyfish?"

"Yeah, je, je, Jellyfish!"

Dragon was carrying a fearsome looking black pool cue with red flames and diamond studded ivory inlays. As he stepped over the ropes, he glanced at the small crowd and started chalking up. Then he turned to me.

"(Humph). So, Nerdburger...I see you brought along enough people here to carry your casket. Going against me at Raul's will be the worst mistake of your non-existent life."

"H, h, how's your sto, stomach Nerd-bur, burger? Hahahaha!!"

I chalked up my cue. I glanced at Brenda, 'the brothers' and then my father. Mr. Connelly and his son stood on the side and watched. Other customers started entering the hall. Brother Star showed Raul the contents of a large envelope behind the front desk. I took a giant gulp.

"What game are we playing?" I asked.

"(Humph). Ever play 9-ball?"

"Yeah."

"(Humph). Well, I figured something different. I want us to play straight pool today. That way I slice your throat nice and quick. Race to seventy-five. Alright?"

"Ok."

We both approached the table for the lag. Dragon won which meant I would break. – As I went to break, I dropped my stick. When I went to pick it up, I smacked my head on the table. Multiple's howling echoed throughout the hall. Brenda fiddled with her necklace. Georgette giggled. The 'brothers' watched attentively. I could see my father sigh and slump slightly in his seat. I re-gathered my composure and re-chalked my cue. I could feel my hands tremble.

"(Humph). Don't scratch Nerdburger. (haha)."

I placed the cue ball on the right side of the table; took my relaxed pool stance; took a deep breathe; put the cue stick directly under my chin; aimed and delivered a gentle hit off the corner ball in the back row with outside english. The cue ball balanced off two rails back to the bottom rail. The stack barely changed. It was the best I could've hoped for.

"(Humph). Hey Jellyfish. I'll bet you another hundred that your man here doesn't get to ten." Knowledge was quiet. The crowd was still. – Dragon called the five ball and hammered the left side of the stack, sinking the five in the top right corner and creating an open table. Dragon's style of play was very aggressive. Dragon had long arms and his fingers looked like octopus tentacles. He walked around the table on each shot and ran out the table in wicked style leaving both the three ball and the cue ball near the center of the table.

Dragon was up 14-0.

I racked the balls as fast as I could and stood back. Dragon easily sank the three in the side pocket, gently rolling the cue off two rails into the stack. The stack didn't move enough for Dragon to have an easy shot. He concentrated and called the seven into the opposite side pocket. Dragon missed and was visibly irritated. However he spread the cluster out, giving me life. – I pocketed the fifteen in the bottom corner. Brenda clapped in her chair. The rest of the crowd was quiet. I sank eight more balls before missing on a cut shot frozen against the rail. Dragon smashed in the rest leaving the twelve and cue balls near the short top rail.

Dragon was up 19- 9.

"(Humph). You know I'm going to cut your head clean off right, Nerdburger?"

"How's ya, ya, your he, head? Hahahaha," shouted Multiple.

I restrained from answering back and stood in the shadows as Dragon chalked up. I thought about Proverbs 18:10- "The name of the LORD is a strong tower; the righteous run to it and are safe."

Dragon sank the twelve putting the cue ball on the right side of the stack. He could have spun the cue ball into the stack but chose not to. He was now thinking defensively. Dragon needed to hit a cushion after making contact in order for the shot to be a legal hit without giving me a shot. That's a true safety. Dragon pondered this dilemma for several seconds and decided to hit the back row ball and tried leaving the cue ball as close to the bottom rail as possible. He needs perfect speed control. He did exactly that, freezing the cue ball against the bottom rail. However he left the six ball near the top corner pocket. I chalked up, elevated my cue and made my shot putting enough english to jar the stack open enough for a combination. I sank ten more shots before missing a cut shot on the two ball. Dragon finished the rest.

Dragon was up 22- 20.

I racked thinking Dragon didn't have a shot because he left the nine ball in front of the stack and the cue ball was behind the stack. I started to chalk up, but Dragon had another idea. He called the eight in the side. The crowd leaned in. He decided to go back to his aggressive shot making capabilities and sank the eight ball, which was buried in the stack, in the side pocket. Raul and Muiltiple cheered. With the table now wide open Dragon ran out the rest of the table. I was quietly impressed and I could feel the pressure.

Dragon was up 36- 20.

I racked again and stood back as Dragon made the one ball in the top left corner spinning the cue ball into the stack. He ran out again.

Dragon was now up 50-20.

"(Humph). Anyone want to take bets on the final score? (humph)."

As Dragon stood over his next shot, he forgot to chalk up and miscued a straight in shot. He didn't hit a cushion either, meaning I had ball in hand. I placed the cue ball behind the head string. My heart rate began to slow down. I started to daydream again. I was in Mr. Evans' basement practicing my shots. The billiards balls looked like the marbles in Mr. Bassford's Science room. I could hear Mr.

Evans' voice. It was equivalent to listening to a song that I wanted to hear over and over again. I knew all the lyrics and steps; all I had to do was dance.

The pockets on the table began to look larger to me. I started seeing the shots more clearly. The crowd became less of a distraction. I ran out. "The Lord is my light and my salvation so why should I be afraid? The Lord is my fortress, protecting me from danger, so why should I tremble?" (Psalm 27:1).

Dragon was up 50- 34, but for the first time in the match Dragon was racking. The crowd perked up some. I could also hear Mr. Evans talking to me.

"Don't forget to chalk up, kid."

I chalked up and lined up my shot. It was a straight in shot. I took a deep breath and slowly exhaled. I made the one all in the side pocket, drawing it back so I could hit a better safety. I rolled the cue ball toward the stack, allowing the cue ball to bounce off the top rail and leave the stack relatively undisturbed. Dragon put extra chalk on his cue and called the four ball in the side. He made it, but the cue ball got kicked by the seven and scratched in the corner pocket.

Dragon lost a point. My father was sitting with his arms folded and was chewing his gum franticly. Raul was joined by his wife and brother Javier at the front desk. Brenda and Georgette were both sitting quietly. 'The brothers' were whispering among themselves on their stools.

Mr. Connelly and his son were watching attentively on the sidelines. I remembered Mr. Evans saying to me... *"Take a breath before every shot, kid."* I took a deep breath and concentrated. I stood up again to relax. I called the seven. Then I went back to the shot and fired. The cue ball rolled into the seven and the seven rolled into its pocket. I exhaled gently. -- I made all fourteen of my shots. Brenda and Mr. Connelly clapped.

Dragon was up 49- 48.

Dragon racked. Javier walked back behind the curtain. Raul made a telephone call and whispered.

"(Humph). You shooting lucky, Nerdburger! It won't last."

The other pool players in Raul's started to gather around and whisper along the wall and sofas. It was still raining outside. I had no shot. The object ball was on the top rail and the cue ball was on the bottom rail. I had a major decision to make: try another cut shot, which has proven to be my Achilles' heel; go aggressive which isn't my game; or go for a safety and put Dragon back at the table, knowing what a great shot maker he is. I paused to take a look at the tip of my cue and chalked up. Mr. Evans kept talking to me.

"A great defense is a great offense, kid."

I called safety and hit the back corner ball sending the cue down table. It almost scratched, but stayed at the edge of the pocket far away from the thirteen ball on the rail. Dragon didn't have a natural angle on the thirteen. Dragon walked around the table twice studying every possible angle and position. Finally he called the four ball which was buried in the stack. The crowd was still. I held my breath. Dragon leaned in and sent balls flying every which way. The four ball fell in. Raul and his wife cheered. The lay out of the table wasn't easy though. There were was a cluster of the twelve, nine and five ball at the side rail. This was wasn't an easy out. Dragon made the eight, one, fifteen, three, two, eleven, and the ten with diabolical skill. Now he had a problem. He needed to make a shot and break open the cluster, but there wasn't a way to do that. Dragon circled and studied the cluster like he was expecting it to give birth. He was attempting a reverse bank on the twelve to go in the corner pocket. He would have great position on the rest of the table if he makes it. Members of the crowd stood up to get a better look. All I wanted was a chance back at the table. Dragon missed. The cluster was broken. I put an emphasis on breathing calmly and walking to the table without looking at the crowd. My heart began to race again. I imagined Mr. Slate yelling in the background. I chalked up. I made the last seven shots on the table.

Dragon was up 56- 55.

Dragon racked. I had an open cut shot on the object ball. I also had to break the stack open. If I missed, the probability of Dragon finishing me off was near 100%. My palms began to sweat. I hadn't made a cut shot the whole match and now I needed to use english on top of that. I tried to slow my breathing. I chalked up. I called the six ball in the corner pocket. The crowd leaned in. -- I made the shot and jarred the stack loose just enough to have an angle on the eight. I ran out the stack!!

I was up 69- 56.

Dragon angrily racked the balls and said...

"(Humph). I bet anyone in here, this nerd chokes!!! He's gonna choke, watch!!"

Chapter 13

Levitation

*T*he crowd was silent as I approached my shot. The seven was open and I had the angle I needed. I called the seven. The four. Then the two. Then the three. Next the fourteen. Finally I had the nine hanging in the pocket. It was a straight in shot. I chalked up. The crowd was on its feet. I took a deep breath and gently rolled the cue ball into the nine. The nine dropped. The crowd went wild. Brenda was ecstatic. My father had the proudest look on his face. 'The brothers' hollered and jumped throughout the pool hall. I walked over to my father and he calmly said...

"You did it, son. You did it."

Mr. Connelly walked over to us and shook my hand and said...

"You really are 'the best'. Great match. Great win."

"Thanks."

Raul handed an envelope to Brother Star and Star handed me a smaller banking envelope from his vest pocket and said...

"Young blood, you did it. I'm proud of you. - Open this when you get home, understand?"

I excused myself from the crowd and walked over to Brenda and Georgette.

"Wow, Bagel Boy! I didn't know you could play like that."

"Please call me Grice."

"Ok... I will...Grice. Grice the Great."

Brenda leaned in and kissed me on my cheek. I smiled.

"See you later, Grice," said Brenda as she smiled. Georgette giggled. I could feel God's hand on my shoulder. I smiled. -- My father grabbed his jacket and we walked out of Raul's together. The two bicycles that were under the canopy were gone and the heavy rain had stopped momentarily. I smiled.

As my father started the Mustang, Knowledge walked up to the passenger side window. I rolled it down.

"G-man," Knowledge shook my hand and nodded with approval.

I smiled and nodded back.

As my father and I rode home together, I smiled. My father smiled, too. Louis Armstrong's "What A Wonderful World" played on the radio. I told my father that I was going to change my major from Electronics to the new Business Entrepreneurship program offered at Northside. He smiled. I wanted to start and run my own pool hall. I wanted to teach ghetto kids the art of playing pool. I wanted to be like Cisero Murphy and... my dad. I wanted to spread God's encouraging word. I wanted to hang the American flag in MY pool hall. – I had a dream. And I smiled. Images of Jennifer Gooden dressed in white danced in my mind. I felt like I was levitating. The rain had stopped and I could see different shades of gray. I closed my eyes and daydreamed some more... and smiled.

Mrs. Brunswick was right.

The LORD is my shepherd, I shall not be in want. He makes me lie down in green pastures, He leads me beside quiet waters, He restores my soul. He guides me in paths of righteousness for his name's sake. Even though I walk through the valley of the shadow of death, I will fear no evil, for you are with me; your rod and your staff, they comfort me. You prepare a table before me in the presence of my enemies. You anoint my head with oil; my cup overflows. Surely goodness and love will follow me all the days of my life, and I will dwell in the house of the LORD forever.

Psalm 23

The end